The Advent Calendar

by
Jeremy Davies

MENIN HOUSE

Menin House is an imprint of
Tommies Guides Military Book Specialists

Gemini House
136-140 Old Shoreham Road
Brighton
BN3 7BD

www.tommiesguides.co.uk

First published in Great Britain by
Menin House Publishers 2014

ISBN 978-1-908336-54-5 (Paperback)
ISBN 978-1-908336-55-2 (Hardback)

Interior design by Vivian @ Bookscribe

Illustrations and cover design by Phill Evans

Printed and bound in Great Britain

CONTENTS

CHAPTER 1
The Accident on the Pass

The world we live in is full of possibilities, chances and choices. Each can lead to a different outcome and many believe that there are infinite parallel universes as a result. We are lucky to live in the one we do, but what if…

20TH DECEMBER 1979

'Easy, easy,' bellowed a booming voice.

The weather was terrible, a gale was blowing and the driving snow was making visibility almost zero. The bearded man was travelling too fast and too high; his face and beard were almost frozen, but he had to keep going, people were depending on him. He could see a row of lights below him in the distance and instinctively he just kept heading in that direction.

Up ahead there was a huge traffic jam, the roads were treacherous and everyone was heading home for Christmas. Stuck right in the middle of the holdup was the Patterson family, parents George and Esther with their three children Joshua, Alex and Anna.

'I knew this was a bad idea,' said Esther. 'Shopping is always chaos this close to Christmas and the weather has made things much, much worse.'

With the schools only a few days from the Christmas break they all knew that the shops would be busy, but the forecast hadn't predicted this crazy weather.

'Don't worry,' said George, 'we've got plenty of time. Let's stick on some Christmas songs!'

They had been in this traffic for nearly an hour and the children were getting restless in the back of the car.

'How long to go now mum?' asked Joshua. He was the impatient one, full of energy and desperate to get home for tea. Esther just turned round and gave him the look. He knew his question was ridiculous, but it was just one of those questions that children seem to ask, along with 'Where are we now?' and 'What time will we get there?'

The family had spent the afternoon shopping for some last minute Christmas presents, but with it getting dark by four and the weather being so bad, they were now stuck in the mother of all queues, barely moving for the last thirty minutes.

Dad dug out his Christmas cassette, blew off the dust and placed it in the player. The selection of Christmas classics partially helped to ease the boredom. Their parents, George and Esther, seemed to be getting more out of the songs than their children as they sang along to 'Frosty the Snowman'. The children were not so impressed and shook their heads with an almost embarrassed disapproval. This time of year was always an excuse for the grown-ups to play cheesy classics and justify them as festive.

Sitting snugly in their overloaded car, the family just needed to wait patiently and eventually they would make it home. However, it wasn't being stuck in traffic that worried Joshua, it was being stuck with his Dad's singing that was the problem!

Up above in the freezing night sky things were getting worse. The bearded man was struggling to control the reins and his frozen hands were failing to grip in the cold.

'Down boys, down,' he yelled, desperate to get onto solid ground, but constantly mindful that he mustn't be spotted.

The trusty reindeer guiding the sled headed down at an acute angle towards the road. One of the harnesses was coming loose on the sled and they needed to land, and quickly. It was almost impossible to see what was ahead of them as the snow was severely impairing their vision. Unbeknown to them they were heading down towards the traffic, but suddenly there was a clearing in the blizzard and the old man pulled on the reins.

'Whoa! Pull up, pull up!' he yelled, as it became frighteningly obvious that they were too low. They were heading straight for the back of a small people carrier.

With all his effort he pulled sharply on the reins. The strain was too much and the left harness came flying loose. The sled lifted slightly and then tilted to the right, scraping across the roof of the people carrier. Out of control they were now heading straight for the moving traffic on the other side of the road. The number 25 bus was coming straight for them. The bus driver had little time to react but swerved sharply to the left and struck an old red phone box before riding up the embankment and tipping in almost slow motion onto its side.

The car behind tried to brake but was too late and ploughed straight into the back of the bus. This signalled a chain reaction of traffic unable to stop in the icy conditions and resulted in them careering into one another.

The sled fared no better, crashing into the embankment and tipping upside down before being dragged skywards again, completely coming free from its strapping and falling down onto the opposite side of the road.

'What was that? What was that?' yelled Joshua. He had heard all the commotion from the back of the car even with his parents' embarrassing singing and was as ever eager to know more.

'Wait here,' said his Dad, 'I'll go take a look.'

George stepped out of the car and made his way back along the road. Most people were out of their cars by now trying to help any injured passengers. The bus was on its side and the passengers were being helped out; some more seriously hurt than others and in need of immediate attention. There was one passenger from the bus who was unconscious. He was dressed in a Santa outfit and the bystanders assumed he must have been heading home from a day's work at the local shopping centre. People gathered around him, concerned about his condition.

'Don't worry,' said the bus driver as he knelt over the poor man, 'help is on its way.'

George looked back towards his car anxiously, knowing only too well that his family had just had a lucky escape. He waved half-heartedly in an attempt to reassure them. George was well known in the town and several of his friends were among the crowd.

'Hey George,' said Tony, the local store manager. 'Did you see what happened?'

'Not from where I was, just heard a bit of a commotion,' he replied.

The bus driver was clearly shaken by what had happened and was desperately trying to make sense of it all.

'All I could see was this thing coming straight for us,' he said. 'I couldn't make out what it was.'

The people carrier, which had been caught up in the accident, had a huge dent across the roof where the sled had caught it. The driver of the vehicle wasn't sure exactly what had hit them.

'Was it a falling tree or some branches being blown by the blizzard?' he asked the driver.

'Could be, I'm really not sure myself,' he replied.

The winds were that strong and the visibility so poor that no one had a decent view of the incident and, as usual, everyone had a theory.

It seemed to take an eternity for the ambulance to arrive. When it did the paramedics rushed over to the man still lying unconscious in the snow. They seemed anxious and acted quickly. The bus driver was clearly shaken and also worried about the condition of the injured man.

'He must have got on the bus at the last stop,' he said. 'I hadn't even noticed him, poor guy.'

'We'll take it from here, he's in safe hands,' said the paramedic in an attempt to reassure the driver.

Accidents are just that, accidents, but it's still difficult for those involved not to feel a sense of responsibility. This was clearly the case for the bus driver, even though his quick reactions had undoubtedly saved further injuries.

The paramedics placed the man on a stretcher and loaded it onto the ambulance. By now other ambulances had arrived, but the other injured people seemed to be fairing a little better and were at least conscious. The ambulance carrying the unconscious man slowly weaved its way between the damaged vehicles and headed off to the hospital its blue, flashing lights reflecting off the white snow.

Just as the lights disappeared into the distance everything seemed to come to a halt. The wind dropped and a strange silence descended all around. Then out of nowhere an eerie cluster of saddening bleats rang out into the still air. It was a noise that Joshua, sitting in the back of the car and peering out of the rear window, would never ever forget.

CHAPTER 2
A Slippery Slope

THURSDAY, 12TH DECEMBER 2014

'Too fast, too fast!' screamed Ethan as he and his big brother Jack sped down the snow-covered hill on their makeshift sledge. He was holding on for all his might but had no confidence in his brother, or their sledge!

'No way,' replied Jack. He was the adrenaline junkie in the family and nothing was too fast or too dangerous for him. The hill was not that steep as it happens and had a nice gradual flattening off at the bottom where their sledge finally came to rest. The whole field was full of children enjoying the snow. Ethan loved this time of year but wasn't quite big enough to be allowed to go sledging alone.

Their sister Abigail was waiting for them at the bottom.

'Did you see us, did you see us Abi?' shouted Ethan excitedly.

'Yes,' she replied, 'you were going so fast.'

'I wanted to go faster,' Ethan said, 'but Jack was too scared.'

Jack laughed to himself but wasn't going to burst Ethan's bubble, he was fourteen now and five years older than his brother. Abigail was the oldest child at fifteen and had been sent by their mum to let the boys know it was time to come home so they could get dry before tea was ready. She hadn't come alone though, Max was with her. Abi was feeling the cold and was desperate to get back, but she couldn't see Max anywhere. She let out a loud whistle and bounding around the corner came Max, struggling to keep his footing in the snowy conditions. It was a comical scene watching this uncoordinated Old English sheepdog slip and slide his way across the field. As he approached them he seemed to be gathering momentum rather than slowing down. The look on the dog's face was comical, a mixture of fear and confusion; he desperately tried to put on the brakes but it was too late. He crashed into Ethan sending them both clattering into the three rough-looking, older boys standing nearby.

'Sorry, sorry, sorry!' said Ethan, as he clambered to his feet brushing off the snow.

The look on the boys' faces said it all; getting knocked to the ground in a heap did little for their reputation. If Ethan had been their size things may have been a little different, but this time they let it go.

Max came over to them looking a little forlorn. Very little Max did these days surprised these three. He was nearly two now, that's almost fourteen in dog years, so he clearly had a little growing up to do yet and had already gained a bit of a reputation for his clumsiness.

Jack and Abi were still laughing, trying their best not to let the other boys see them.

'That was legendary,' said Jack. 'Wish I had filmed that!'

'Shut up,' said Ethan, clearly a little embarrassed.

'Come on you two,' said Abi, 'Mum said we need to get back.'

The three set off for home. The walk was about ten minutes in total and they came off the field and headed back down towards the town. The view from the path down to the town was magnificent, the snow had made the setting become almost magical. The seaside town, sixty miles or so south of London, was set in a picturesque cove and the landscape was dotted with imperious willow trees. With the heavy snowfall of recent days it had been transformed into a winter wonderland. It was getting on for four o'clock by now and as the winter clocks had gone back some weeks ago it was starting to get dark. The small, homely houses of the town were well lit and made sure people were able to make their way about in the evening.

Ethan was first in through the back door slipping his wellies off and sprinting through the hall and up the stairs, leaving a trail of snow that was falling off his coat.

'Ethan!' yelled his mother. 'Take your coat off next time.'

He was so desperate for a hot shower that he had forgotten the rules. The other two came in and left their outdoor clothes where they should be. Then came Max, shaking himself dry in the kitchen. Mum was not impressed as she gave him the knowing look.

'Did you boys have a good time?' she asked.

'Oh Mum, it was hilarious,' said Jack, barely able to contain himself. 'Max totally wiped Ethan out, you should have seen it.'

'That bloody dog,' she said. 'He's a disaster waiting to happen. Now go get yourself cleaned up.'

Abigail went to stand in front of the fireplace to warm up, desperately trying to get the blood circulating through her hands again. Tea was going to be ready soon and the three of them still had to shower and change before they sat down. Jack made his way upstairs to get ready for the shower and Abi stayed downstairs to help her Mum with the tea.

CHAPTER 3
At Home

THURSDAY, 12TH DECEMBER

Abigail was the last to get showered as usual, the boys insisted she went last every time. Ethan was in his bedroom just replying to a text from a friend when he heard the front door go downstairs. His Dad had just arrived home, he'd been away for a couple of days and Ethan had missed him. He jumped up and ran across the landing and down the stairs. In typical Ethan fashion he appeared to miss the last two stairs and came crashing down on the hallway floor in a heap.

'Hi mate,' said his father, 'have you been on the drink again?'

Ethan laughed as he climbed slowly to his feet and gave his Dad a hug.

'Is that you Josh?' called Mum from the kitchen.

'Yes darling,' he replied.

'How was the road?' she asked. Josh's route to work involved some difficult terrain, particularly in the current snowy conditions. The 'pass', a stretch of road to the north of the town, was particularly hazardous and had seen many an accident over the years. Josh in particular still had vivid memories of being a small boy in the back of his father's car during the crash of 1979.

'I've seen worse,' he responded as he hung his coat on the bannister at the bottom of the stairs.

His timing was impeccable as tea was just about to be served. He picked Ethan up and carried him to the kitchen where they sat down around the dining table ready for tea. Mum yelled upstairs for the other two. Jack and Abi came down and gave their father a hug before quickly sitting down for tea. Clearly their bellies were far more important than welcoming their father home.

The family happily tucked into Mum's tea. She was the best cook and this was the one time the house was silent as they all were too busy filling their faces to chatter.

'So what did you three get up to after school today?' asked Dad. 'You've got three weeks off school now, I don't know how your mother will cope with you under her feet for these winter holidays.' He chuckled to himself as Mm gave him 'the stare' across the table.

'Actually, I'll probably hardly see them with all the time they spend on that bin lid they call a sledge,' she replied.

Their father had a strange look on his face like someone who was trying to remember something.

'I wonder?' he said.

'Wonder what?' said Mum.

'Well, I was just thinking if I still had that old sledge of mine in the attic,' he replied.

The boys looked up and then at each other, clearly excited as they had struggled to find anything decent to use for a sled and were still using an old plastic bin lid. Ethan had grown rather attached to it and believed it looked cool strapped across his back using the string he had attached to it.

'Well, it must be almost thirty years since I've used it. Once we've finished here we can go for a look up in the attic,' said Dad.

They had lived in the house for almost fifteen years now and they were a typical family. Mum and Dad both worked, Mum as an assistant at the local school and Dad in the city nearby. He was always home at weekends but occasionally had to work away during the week. Abigail was in her GCSE year and was expecting great results. Jack, well, he was bright but spent nearly all his time playing sports. As for Ethan he was into everything – questions, questions, questions – was all you got from him, but as the baby of the family the others looked after him well.

Mum and Dad were sitting down on the sofa with a cup of tea catching up on the last few days. Abi was on her iPad chatting with friends. Jack, well, he was as usual trawling through the Sky sports channels looking for something to watch. Ethan though was growing impatient.

'Dad can we look for the sledge?' he asked.

'Let your father finish his tea,' Mum said.

'No, that's OK,' said dad. 'Jack, you coming?'

'Two minutes,' he replied, unable to drag himself away from the sports news channel.

Ethan was too small to reach the chord to pull the attic ladder down so his father lifted him up so he could reach. He pulled a little too hard and the stairs came flying down; they both just got out of the way in time. Ethan sniggered.

Ethan clambered quickly up the steps into total darkness.

'Dad?' he said, hoping his father was beside him as he wasn't a fan of the dark. He was relieved when his Dad pulled the chord to switch the light on. Up in the attic there was stuff everywhere. Ethan hadn't been up there for ages and he was shocked by just how much 'stuff' there was. Despite the amount crammed into the loft it was all pretty well organised, Mum had a bit of a thing for tidiness. There were so many boxes, where did they start? They were busy looking when Jack, who'd crept up unnoticed, thought he'd found it under some blankets.

'Is this it?'

'I didn't hear you come up here,' said Dad.

'I was in stealth mode,' replied Jack sarcastically.

'Smart Alec,' snapped his father as he came over to take a closer look.

'Don't be daft, that's a rocking horse,' he said.

All Jack had seen were the two rockers across the bottom of the horse that looked a little like the runners of a sledge. Alongside the horse were a few large boxes marked with the word 'Christmas'. He had a quick peek inside and saw some crazy looking items – tinsel, glitter and all sorts of bright colours. A little confused by the box Jack's face carried a puzzled look.

'Here it is,' said Dad at the far end of the attic.

Jack and Ethan ran over to take a look. It really was a proper sledge made from wood with two sleek looking blades and a leather set of reigns. It was red with green blades and a holly pattern around the seat.

'This looks great Dad,' said a delighted Ethan, 'much better than my shield sled.' That was the name he'd given the bin lid.

'Let's get it down. Can you put the loft hatch back Jack?' asked Dad, who, along with Ethan, took the sledge down the stairs and into the lounge for a closer look.

Jack was about to climb back down when he remembered the box he had seen. He dropped the box down through the hatch onto the landing and then climbed down and closed the hatch behind him.

Downstairs Dad was showing the sledge to the family, who all seemed quite impressed.

'I want first go, I want first go!' said Ethan. They all knew that if he didn't get first go he'd be a nightmare for the next few days, so they promised that tomorrow he'd get to use the sledge. Behind them Jack was sitting at the table looking through the box he had found.

'What are these Dad?' Jack said as he pulled a few decorations out, 'and who's this?'

Jack was holding a small Father Christmas decoration. Dad looked at Mum with a slightly worried expression on his face.

'Those are decorations son and that man is Father Christmas'.

'Who's Father Christmas?' asked Abi.

'He's just an old man that used to visit every December when we were children,' replied Mum.

'But what are all these decorations?' asked Jack.

Mum and Dad appeared to be bracing themselves for a barrage of questions. It appeared they knew what was coming.

'He used to bring us presents and we used to decorate the house to make it nice for him and to celebrate Christmas'.

'Christmas?' said Ethan with a puzzled look on his face.

'Yes, that's the time of year when Father Christmas, or Santa as we used to call him, came to visit to bring us all presents. We used to love it,' said Mum.

'But why don't we get presents?' asked Ethan.

'Well, Santa stopped coming a long time ago. We're not sure why but I suppose he was getting old and needed to stop travelling. Don't worry we're going on holiday in a week so we'll make our own fun,' Dad said. 'Now let me get this old stuff back into the attic.'

Jack looked at Abi, they were both clearly dissatisfied by their parents' answers but could see that they were a little uneasy about answering questions so decided not to push the matter any further.

Later that evening when the three children had gone to bed Mum and Dad were talking in the kitchen.

'Do you think they will want to know more?' asked Dad.

'I'm not sure,' replied Mum. 'It's such a shame they'll never get to see Christmas as we knew it.'

'I know, but remember how upset people were when we waited all those years.'

The Christmas Josh and his wife knew as children stopped in 1979. The local people carried on the tradition of decorating their houses, putting stockings out, singing carols and much more for another five or six years in the hope that Santa would return and Christmas would be Christmas once again. However, each year they became more and more disappointed, until finally everyone agreed that they had to stop pinning their hopes on Father Christmas and accept that Christmas was over for good. It was a heart-breaking time for communities across the world and one by one they agreed to try and forget about Christmas and avoid any more unnecessary disappointment.

'Don't worry though,' said Dad, 'we'll make sure this trip is fun, and we'll make sure every year we do something special.'

Mum had a tear in her eye, clearly the memory of Christmas was enough to upset her and Dad could see this. He leaned across to give her a hug.

Upstairs Jack was in Abi's room.

'What do you make of this Christmas thing Abs?' he said.

'A bit weird,' she replied. 'Mum was looking a bit upset don't you think.'

'Yes, I saw that. Not sure what to think to be honest... anyway, goodnight,' said Jack as he headed off to his bed.

That night Mum, Dad and the boys slept soundly. As for Abigail, she was online until about four o'clock in the morning searching for anything to do with Christmas. Strangely, wherever she looked, whatever she typed, drew no results whatsoever, it was as if this Christmas thing had never existed. The only real story of Willow Cove dating back to 1979 was that of the awful crash on the pass which her father Josh, then a small child, and her grandfather George, had been unfortunate enough to witness.

Finally, exhausted by both the late hour and her unsuccessful research, Abi fell asleep.

CHAPTER 4
The Discovery

FRIDAY, 13TH DECEMBER

'Come on Jack, come on Jack,' screamed Ethan.

He was jumping up and down on Jack's bed, desperate to get out in the snow on his 'new' sledge.

'Get lost,' yelled Jack. 'It's too early.' It was ten to nine, and a day off for Jack.

'That's what you think,' said Ethan who whisked off Jack's duvet and ran across the landing and downstairs with it trailing behind him.

'Aaarrgghhh!' shouted Jack in frustration. He had no choice now but to get up, so he trudged across to the bathroom with a resigned look on his face.

Downstairs Ethan was so excited about the new sledge and was waiting impatiently for Jack.

'Now you be careful up there today and make sure you take care of him,' Mum said to Jack as he came into the kitchen looking like a zombie.

'This is too early,' he said pulling one of his wellies onto the wrong foot. Mornings were not really Jack's strong point. As for Abi she rarely got out of bed before midday during the holidays, so when she rushed through the kitchen and out of the door with barely a goodbye it made everyone stop with shock.

'I wonder where she's going?' said Jack.

'No idea,' said Mum, 'I don't think she's working until eleven.'

Abi had a part-time job for the holidays working in a local café down by the cove called Terra Nova. Typically she was always looking for work, nothing was too much for Abi.

Jack and Ethan left the house and headed towards the field. Today was a beautiful day, crystal clear with the sun shining. The path up to the field was tricky as snow had fallen again overnight and it was quite tricky to see where the sides of the path finished. There was quite a drop off to one side so the boys figured as long as they stayed as central as possible it would be OK. The walk to the field took longer than expected and by the time they arrived it was already busy, even at that time in the morning.

A few of Ethan's friends saw him coming and saw the sledge he was pulling behind him, rushing over for a closer look.

'Where did you get that?' said Billy, a giant of a nine-year-old who came to the field all the time but never rode a sledge. He simply stood at the bottom watching and laughing.

'It's Dad's old sledge,' replied Ethan.

'Nice,' said Billy. 'Looks like it will bomb down the hill.'

'Well, shall we find out?' Jack asked.

'Wait a minute,' said a voice.

It was one of the three boys Ethan had smashed into yesterday. All three were there and looking at the sledge.

'You're the idiot with the daft dog and now you've got a daft sledge to match!' he said laughing and the other two joined in.

'It's quicker than your plastic rubbish,' said Ethan.

'Really?' he responded. 'Is that a challenge?'

'Yes, it damn well is,' interrupted Jack. He was always up for a challenge; it was like a red rag to a bull. Ethan turned to his brother with a worried look on his face, he knew that once Jack was challenged there was no going back.

'Let's go,' Jack said staring at one of the boys. Then he remembered Ethan had been promised first go, so he turned to his brother and said, 'Sorry I forgot you have to go first.'

'That's OK,' said one of the boys, 'ours is a two-man sled, so is yours, so let's race!'

Ethan whispered to Jack, 'Are you sure about this?' Jack shrugged his shoulders and they started the walk up the hill.

Abigail had left the house in a hurry that morning and was heading into town. She was confused as to why nothing had come back on her Internet searches regarding Christmas, so she had decided to go through the old archives in the library. The town library was in the square in the centre of town, an old, impressive building that in all honesty Abi had hardly visited over the years. The school library and the computer seemed to provide everything she needed. The town was relatively quiet, it was still early after all and with the inches of snow that had fallen overnight it was pretty hard to get about.

Abi figured that her best bet would be to take a look at the old newspaper articles from years ago. She asked the clerk at the desk where they were stored and then headed downstairs to do some digging.

The library was deathly quiet and Abi felt uncomfortable even opening and closing files such was the silence. She started with the 1980s but there was nothing in 1989, nothing in 1988, nothing in fact until she got to 1984. The newspaper had a story on 'Moving on from Christmas' and Abi was immediately drawn in. As she researched further and further back she began to learn more and more about Christmas and its traditions.

It was clear that it was a time of year that people loved and that it had made millions of people across the world extremely happy. She was stunned at all the various traditions and meanings Christmas had and was amazed that she had never heard of such a wonderful part of her country's history.

Abi couldn't help but experience the sadness that people obviously felt since Christmas had ended all those years ago. She spent over an hour making notes so she could tell Jack and Ethan what she had found. She thought to herself how awful 1979 must have been to the local community, with the awful crash on the pass and the ending of Christmas, how sad. Time had flown while she was searching and as Abi looked at her watch she realised she was going to be late if she didn't leave soon. She quickly packed her stuff away, put her notes in her bag and headed for work.

Back in the field Ethan and Jack had pulled the sledge right up to the highest point of the hill. The two boys alongside them looked determined to win the race back down; on the count of three they would go.

'One, two…' counted Jack, but before he could get to three the others had pushed off. 'Cheats,' he thought to himself, but still he wanted to win, so off they went.

It was crystal clear from the second they pushed off the sledge was crazily fast. Within a few seconds they had caught up with the other two and were speeding away. Ethan was cheering loudly, Jack was almost laughing with shock, the crazy kind of laugh that you get on a roller coaster, half scream, half laugh.

'Woohooo,' yelled Ethan, this was one race that was virtually won. The field started to flatten out near the bottom but something was beginning to worry both Jack and Ethan, they weren't slowing down at all! In fact even a small slope was encouraging the sledge to speed up. It suddenly dawned on the two boys that this sledge wasn't going to stop.

'Jump, jump!' yelled Jack. Ethan by now had his eyes closed and was holding on with all his might. Jack's instructions were too late, the sledge flashed in between the people at the bottom of the slope and causing some of them to dive for safety. It then crashed through the fence at the end of the field, sped across the narrow road and fell down a steep embankment. Even though they were travelling at such a speed the crash itself seemed to be in slow motion. Ethan luckily was thrown clear and simply rolled down the embankment coming to a rest in a huge snowdrift. Jack wasn't so lucky, he was determined to hold onto the sledge and went all the way to the bottom of the small valley, luckily coming to a halt on a small ledge.

That was too close for comfort, he thought, but just as he gathered his bearings and was thinking he'd had a lucky escape, the ground beneath him gave way and he fell about twelve feet into some sort of cave.

'Jack, Jack!' screamed Ethan as he scrambled down the hill looking for his brother. The people in the field were a distant memory now as they had travelled quite some distance. Ethan was worried, they were too far from help and there was no sign of Jack.

'I'm OK,' shouted Jack. Ethan felt instant relief and the crazy panic subsided. No more what 'ifs' ran through his head.

'I'm in here.' Ethan approached the hole where Jack had fallen and stuck his head over.

'Jack, you there?' he asked.

'Yes, I'm in here,' he replied.

'Are you hurt? Are you bleeding?' Ethan asked. It was clear he was upset, almost panicking.

'I think I'm OK,' Jack said.

'What about the sledge?' asked Ethan. The second he said it he cringed that he'd even asked!

'The bloody sledge,' Jack yelled. Looking around him he could see it was actually still in one piece, but that wasn't the point.

The cave was cold and damp and he wondered how long it had been here and if he was alone. He tried to look around but his eyes had yet to adjust to the darkness.

'Ethan,' he said, 'take your coat and jumper off and tie them together to make a kind of rope. I'll try and see if there's anything here I can use.'

Ethan quickly took his coat and jumper off, leaving him with just his base layer. He got to work on tying a secure knot he'd recently learned in Scouts. Meanwhile, Jack was starting to explore the cave, when he noticed a strange radiance coming from under some rocks and branches. He approached the pile and could now clearly see a golden glow coming from underneath the rubble. He started to clear the branches away and saw a dust-covered book glowing like nothing he had ever seen before.

'Ethan I think I've found something,' he said.

'What is it?' replied Ethan, who then rushed over to the hole. In his excitement he had moved far too quickly and slid on the snow beside the hole and fell straight through, down into the cave.

Jack struggled not to laugh. Even though it meant they could be stuck, he couldn't help but see the funny side of Ethan's clumsiness. Fortunately, as Jack's sight improved he could clearly see it was possible to climb up the side of the cave quite easily to reach the opening.

They both started to clear the branches and stones from the book. When it was clear they stood back, almost in shock, staring down at it. Now that they had moved everything out of the way, the glow coming from the book was so powerful it almost lit the whole cave. They looked at each other in astonishment. Jack went over to the book and picked it up. Other than the powerful glow it was no different from any other large book; it felt the same and weighed the same, but strangely it wouldn't open.

'Let's get this home,' Jack said.

The boys took a while to get the sledge from the cave as the 'easy' climb up the side of the rock wasn't so easy carrying a sledge. Ethan climbed up first and leant over so Jack could pass up the sledge. Jack then climbed back down to fetch the book which he tucked inside his jacket and then managed to climb out himself. Once they were outside Ethan put his coat back on but used his jumper to wrap up the book, the glow was still visible but not quite so strong. They looked around, no one was in sight, in fact nothing familiar was in sight. They were going to have to drag themselves back up the small valley and find the path home, quite a trek lay ahead.

'That was mental,' said Ethan.

'I know, crazy. I thought I was a goner,' replied Jack. 'I don't think we should tell anyone about this book yet though Ethan, let's try and figure it out first. What do you say?'

'OK, it's up to you Jack,' replied Ethan showing as always an undying trust for his big brother. They got their possessions together and started the difficult journey home. Jack was worried that someone would spot the glow coming from underneath Ethan's jumper, so he placed the bundle inside his coat to make sure they could get back home without it being spotted.

It was just before lunchtime when the boys finally arrived home, they were absolutely shattered.

'Hello, you two,' said Mum, looking puzzled.

'Why are you home so early?' she asked.

'Umm... it's a bit too busy up the field and Ethan's not feeling the best,' replied Jack hesitantly. Ethan looked at his brother with a quizzical expression.

'Yeah,' responded Ethan quickly with a husky tone, clearly trying to sound as ill as possible.

'Oh well, I suppose you're best off in the warm,' replied Mum.

Ethan removed his coat and placed it on the hanger. Jack was clearly hesitant to do this, worried about exposing their 'find'. He quickly turned and headed for the stairs with Ethan following like a tail.

'Coat!' shouted mum.

Jack quickly removed the book wrapped in Ethan's jumper passing it to his brother at the foot of the stairs before heading back to the kitchen to remove his coat.

'Sorry Mum,' he said.

'You boys, you've got the memories of goldfish,' she said laughing.

Jack sprinted up the stairs to his bedroom where Ethan was waiting. Ethan had placed the book on Jack's bed and had started to unwrap it.

'What is it?' he asked Jack.

'I've no idea,' he replied. As he started to wipe the dust off the book it became clear very quickly that this was something that had some special meaning. The book was almost magical in appearance, full of colour: greens, reds and gold. It was decorated with some amazing patterns, the like of which neither of the boys had ever seen before. As Jack wiped the top of the book clear with his sleeve two words appeared, 'ADVENT Calendar'. Clearly this was the title of the book, but it had no meaning to the boys.

'It's a calendar,' said Jack clearly confused.

They knew exactly what a calendar was, but the word 'Advent' was new to them.

'What does Advent mean Jack?' asked Ethan, sure that his big brother would know.

'Dunno,' replied Jack. 'Perhaps something to do with adventure.'

Clearly the boys would need to do a little research on this word to try and make sense of it. They decided to hide the book away until later on, but as Jack picked it up he noticed another set of letters running down the spine of the book. These were unlike the heading of the book, moveable letters, not unlike a combination lock, but this time with letters instead of numbers. There were ten in total, two sets of five.

'A combination?' said Jack, holding the book for Ethan to see. Just then Mum called them both for lunch. Jack quickly wrapped the book up and slid it under his bed before heading down for lunch.

After lunch the boys settled down to watch the afternoon movie. This was one of the bonuses of the school holidays, the television channel always played movies.

Mum was busy as always, she never seemed to stop during the day, it was either cooking or cleaning; the boys were always surprised at how she never seemed to relax.

'Come watch the film,' said Ethan. If anyone was going to persuade Mum to have a break it was her 'baby'.

'Oh, all right, just for a bit,' replied Mum as she came through to join them.

They were nearing the end of the film when Abi arrived home.

'It's freezing!' she whimpered as she removed her gloves and coat.

'How was work?' asked Mum.

Jack paused the film, he couldn't stand people talking while he was trying to listen to the television. Mum got up and went through to the kitchen to catch up with Abi.

'Mum!' Jack shouted. 'What about the film?'

'You carry on,' she said. Jack hated that, why would people watch half a film, things like that really frustrated him. Nevertheless, the boys carried on watching. It wasn't long before the film had finished and Ethan had been itching to ask Jack a question.

'Are we going to show Abi?' he asked.

'Don't know,' replied Jack. 'I'm not sure.' Ethan looked a little uneasy with this. Keeping secrets had never been his strong point but he was going to try his best. Just then Abi came through and plonked herself down on the sofa.

'Guess where I've been?' she asked.

'Work,' said Jack flippantly.

'Yes, but where else?'

'The sweet shop!' shouted Ethan with an over-excited look on his face.

'No, you clowns, I've been in the library,' she declared. The boys looked at each other, clearly puzzled as to why it should concern them.

'I've been looking at that Christmas thing Mum and Dad were talking about,' she said. The boys suddenly sat up and took notice. Last night's revelation had clearly interested them and they were eager to know more.

'Let's go upstairs and I'll show you what I found out,' said Abi as she got up from the sofa.

Upstairs in Abi's room she sat down by her computer reached into her bag and pulled out her notes. She repeated the story of Christmas to the boys who sat there in silence, which was a first for these two and clearly demonstrated the magnetism the story held over them. Abigail as always was thorough with her notes and was able to relay the story with as much depth as possible, although there did seem to be a lack of information available online and in normal resources, in fact even the library was a little short of any resources.

'That's a weird story Abs,' said Jack. 'Have you talked more to Mum and Dad?'

'No,' she replied. 'I thought I'd look it up myself, although that's not been easy,' she added. The boys couldn't understand why the Internet carried so little information on this 'Christmas' thing and were almost dubious of the whole story.

Abi and Jack were discussing how they could talk to Mum and Dad about the subject without upsetting them again. They definitely needed a new approach. Ethan, however, was bored and had started rummaging through Abi's notes when he suddenly gasped!

'Abi, what does this mean?' he said, looking strangely at Jack.

'Let me see,' she replied, taking the note from Ethan.

'Oh, that says Advent Calendar, it was a kind of tradition I think,' she said. 'Let me take a look,' she added sifting through her notes.

'Here it is,' she said turning to a page in her notes. 'The original Advent Calendar was thought to have belonged to Santa Claus. He used it as a form of diary throughout the Advent period, which was the period running up until Christmas. Laypeople mimicked the calendar by using more basic versions to count down the days until Christmas,' she read.

'Jack?' said Ethan, with a desperate look on his face,

'Ssh,' replied Jack sharply, clearly frustrated at Ethan's lack of subtlety.

By now Abi had become suspicious.

'What is it? What's the big secret?' she asked, totally unaware of the magnitude of the boy's 'secret'.

Ethan's problem with secrets had surfaced, although this was his sister and it seemed daft to keep it from her.

'Show her Jack,' he pleaded.

'Show me what?' asked an intrigued Abi.

'Ethan!' said a clearly irritated Jack. There was then a pause before he continued

'OK, but you can't tell anyone,' he said, looking seriously at Abi. 'You promise?'

'What are you going on about?' she replied clearly confused.

'Promise!' insisted Jack.

'Yeah, yeah,' said Abi nonchalantly, clearly unaware of what she was about to be shown. Jack led them through to his room where he slowly dragged the covered book from underneath his bed and peeled back the layers to reveal this almost treasure-like object to Abi. Her face was a picture, mouth agape and eyes wide as saucers, it appeared to be an eternity before she blinked and even longer before she spoke.

'Where... what... when!' stuttered Abi, barely able to put a sentence together.

Jack went on to tell Abi the whole story of the sledging incident, still laughing at the point where Ethan fell through the hole. It clearly had something to do with this 'Christmas' thing and was something that needed investigating. Abi pawed over the book looking at every little detail. She was amazed by its beauty and confused as to how it was glowing so brightly. Jack pointed out the combination lock and together they tried to solve the puzzle. Clearly there was a password, but how could they solve it?

Out in the back garden Max could see this mysterious glow coming from Jack's bedroom window and was going berserk, barking like a lunatic. Mum was shouting at him to shut up, but there was no stopping him. She finally opened the door and he ran straight through the house, snow flying everywhere, and ran straight upstairs and started scratching at Jack's door.

The three of them jumped as they heard Max and quickly Jack covered up the book and slid it back under the bed before letting the dog in. Max jostled between the three of them paying them all as much attention as possible, clearly the poor animal had been worried about his friends and was keen to ensure they were OK.

'You crazy dog,' said Abi with a sense of relief as she patted him furiously.

'That was close,' sighed Jack.

'Let's leave it for now, we'll try and find out more tomorrow,' he said.

The three of them returned to the living room to sit in front of the fire and watch TV. Clearly there was unfinished business upstairs, but there was very little they could today. It was dark and the library was shut so there was no chance of doing further investigating.

Dad arrived home and they sat down for dinner as usual. The three children were unusually quiet, deep in their own thoughts. Mum and Dad said little, they were glad of the peace and quiet. The evening passed by without incident and before they knew it, it was bedtime for Ethan, then later for the other two.

'The kids OK?' asked Dad, clearly a little puzzled by the relative peace of this normally bouncing house.

'Yes, I think so,' replied Mum. 'Just a little tired out from all the sledging, or working in Abi's case.'

'Oh, well, I suppose we mustn't grumble, just can't see the peace lasting!' laughed Dad.

CHAPTER 5
The Cave

SATURDAY MORNING, 14TH DECEMBER

Upstairs the boys were sound asleep, but Abi, well, she was wide awake, full of questions and thoughts. She listened diligently for her parents to come to bed and even longer for them to go to sleep. Once she was sure they were sound asleep she started to get dressed. First she put her base layer on and then her waterproofs. She crept across the landing and into Jack's room.

'Jack, Jack,' she whispered, but got no response.

She started to push him gently and finally he started to stir.

'What… What?' he said still clearly confused and half asleep.

'Let's go,' she said.

'Go where?' he replied. By now he had seen that Abi was dressed for the outside.

'The cave!' she said excitedly.

Jack sat up, yes it was the middle of the night, yes he was half asleep, but this whole saga had him gripped and he started to dress.

'OK, OK, but what about Ethan?' he asked, as he ruffled his hair attempting to speed up his wakening.

'I'll go get him,' said Abi slipping quietly out of the room and next door to Ethan's. Jack took a few minutes to get ready and searched his room for his torch. By the time he found it Abi had returned with a weary-looking Ethan, who was still clearly half asleep and not sure what was going on.

'We need to be very quiet,' said Abi and with that the three of them crept across the landing and slowly down the stairs remembering to avoid the bottom step which was ridiculously creaky. Once in the kitchen the three of them started to put on their outdoor shoes and coats. All of a sudden they heard the stairs creak, they all looked at each other, they were clearly about to be caught out. The kitchen door opened slowly. Who was it? Mum or Dad they thought. Then they heard a familiar pant, Max! The three sighed in unison, but they knew that if they walked out without him Max would go mad and surely wake their parents up. So Abi took his lead off the hook by the back door and gave it to Ethan.

'You bring him, or he'll wake them up,' she said.

Ethan knew she was right and slipped the lead over the now over-excited dog who was delighted with the prospect of a walk.

It was cold and crisp outside and the sky was crystal clear. Clearly the walk was out of the ordinary but if more people could see the amazing conditions, they too would take some early morning walks. Ethan was still tired and was leaning on Max as opposed to walking with him and Abi's decision to let him walk the dog now made sense. Jack was leading the way but as yet wasn't using the torch. The town was relatively well lit and he didn't want to draw any unwanted attention to the group so he kept the torch off until they were out of sight.

The way down to the cave was totally off the beaten track and a little confusing for Jack. Ethan was little use with directions and Jack wasn't finding it easy to guide the way. They seemed to be walking for quite some time and Abi was starting to lose her patience as they appeared to be going round in circles.

'Jack are you lost?' asked Abi.

'Just trying to work it out,' he replied with a puzzled look on his face.

'I think we need to go further down,' he said.

Jack was right, with the speed of the new sledge and the steepness of the hill he hadn't realised just how far down the valley they had been carried. The three headed downhill and sure enough as Jack shone the torch across the floor of the valley he could see the small ledge where his sledge had come to rest before crashing down into the cave.

'This way,' he said hurriedly, clearly excited that he had discovered the cave once again.

His confidence was a relief to Abi who was starting to think they were lost. The four of them approached the cave slowly, Ethan in particular, he was still wary of the last time! Looking down into the cave it was impossible to see anything, the torch simply lit up an empty floor.

'How can we get down safely?' asked Abi.

'This way,' replied Jack, 'there's a pretty easy climb down.'

Jack went first and Abi followed. Ethan was staying outside with Max, he didn't want to leave the dog alone and had volunteered to keep watch. Once inside Jack shone his torch on the area where they had found the book, but in honesty there wasn't much to see, just a pile of old rubble. Abi wasn't discouraged, she took the torch from Jack and started to move around the cave.

It was bitterly cold and Jack was jogging on the spot in an attempt to keep warm. Abi was oblivious to the elements as she scoured the cave looking for anything of note, but nothing stood out. Suddenly she felt a smack on the back of her head and snow flew past her cheeks. Looking round she could see Jack looking around whistling nonchalantly, his hand still covered in the leftovers of the snowball he had just launched at her.

'Idiot,' she said.

'You're the idiot,' he replied, turning to gather more snow from the huge pile behind him, before once again pelting it at Abi.

This time, though, Abi was prepared, although you would never have known it. The snowball was heading straight for her face but she didn't move, in fact she just took the full force without flinching, simply wiping the snow from her face and staring back at Jack with a strange look on her face. Jack was confused.

'Abs?' he said, unsure of what was going on. Abi simply lifted her hand and pointed at Jack, or at least that's what he thought. When Jack had taken the snow from the pile behind him he had disturbed something. The majority of the snow had all fallen to the ground revealing the most amazing carriage that Abi had ever seen, regal in appearance and quite simply the most astonishing sight.

Jack turned slowly and then took a few steps backwards.

'What the...?' he said.

'What have you found, what have you found?' asked Ethan, who's head was now hanging down through the opening above.

There was a delay as both Abi and Jack weren't sure themselves exactly what they had just discovered.

'Not sure,' replied Jack, who, along with Abi, started to remove more and more of the snow, exposing what appeared to be a giant sledge. It seemed merely seconds before they had cleared the snow entirely and both stood back to examine their discovery. Abi rifled through her clothes before pulling out her mobile phone and stepping back to take a photo.

'What shall we do now?' asked Jack. It was obvious they couldn't move the enormous sled, but what were they supposed to do with their discovery? Should they need to tell someone, or should they keep it a secret, thought Abi?

'Let's cover the cave up somehow,' she said. 'We don't want anyone else finding this.' Clearly this was a major discovery and fortunately the position of the cave really was off the beaten track and very unlikely to be discovered. Abi took a few more photos before they both climbed out of the cave. Before they left they laid a few branches over the entrance in an attempt to hide their discovery.

'Let's get back,' said Abi, 'I need to get some sort of sleep before work.'

The three of them headed back up the hill before reaching the top of the path that led them back down to the village. They must have been out longer than they thought because as they approached the village they could see a couple of houses with their lights on. It was, however, still early enough for Mum and Dad to still be asleep and fortunately they managed to walk through the village unnoticed and got back home and into bed without waking their parents.

CHAPTER 6
Solving the Riddle

SATURDAY, 14TH DECEMBER

'Jack, get up you're late!' yelled Mum from downstairs. Jack jumped up quickly, 'Late?' he thought, 'what for?' Then it dawned on him, football!

His team had a game that morning, kick-off was at eleven and it was now already ten past ten. The late night had taken its toll on Jack, but that wasn't exactly an excuse he could give his Mum. He quickly started to get dressed before running downstairs and through to the kitchen where his mother was waiting.

'What time do you call this?' she asked. 'You're too late for breakfast now, just have this quickly or you'll be too weak to play,' she said handing over a small breakfast bar. Jack hated them but it was his own fault he had missed breakfast and he did need something inside him. His boots were outside the front door and really in a poor state, but he had no time to do anything about it. He quickly slapped them together a few times to clear the mud that had formed a crust between the studs, before putting them in his kit bag and jumping into the car while Mum shouted goodbye to the other two.

Abi was still in bed but was working at twelve o'clock, only doing the lunchtime shift. She had arranged to drop Ethan off at the football before heading in to work. Abi was always pretty punctual and would need little help in getting herself and Ethan ready in time.

The journey down to the football club was a slow one due to the tricky condition of the roads. Luckily the boys played their games on the astro turf this time of year so at least they were guaranteed a game. They were last to arrive, all the others were there and the away team were just getting off the bus. Jack's coach was talking to his opposite number. He looked over to Jack and just tilted his head, clearly telling him to get to the dressing room with his teammates to change.

Back at home Abi had managed to get Ethan out of bed and made him a hearty breakfast. She was just getting her coat on, ready to leave.

'What are we going to do about the book?' asked Ethan.

'I've got an idea Eth,' replied Abi.

'We'll talk with Jack when we get back this afternoon and decide then, just get your coat on, we need to head off now,' she said.

Abi had been racking her brains about what they should do and had come up with a plan, but it needed both Jack and Ethan to help. Once her shift was over and everyone was home she would go through her idea with the boys.

They headed down through the village and past the square before heading down towards the beach and to the Leisure Centre. Ethan could hear the cheer from the crowds as they approached the football field.

'They've already started,' he said in a disappointed voice and started to pick up his pace.

'Careful,' said Abi, 'it's pretty slippery down there.' Ethan didn't take a blind bit of notice, he was in a hurry and nothing could stop him. Ethan had always looked up to Jack and loved to watch the football games. They arrived at the pitch and Jack, as usual, was in the thick of the action, sliding in to take almost every challenge with reckless abandon.

'Typical Jack,' sighed Abi as she watched a few minutes of the action before leaving Ethan with Mum and heading off for work.

'Have fun,' said Mum. Abi turned with a quizzical look. 'Fun at work?' she thought, her mother's dry sense of humour was wasted on her.

The football was such a release for Jack, he loved his sport and loved the challenge it brought. He was always fully committed to winning and gave everything for his team. This afternoon was no exception as an all-action performance helped his team to a comfortable 3-0 win. Some of Ethan's friends from school were also watching the game and stayed around for a kick about after the game while the teams showered and changed.

Jack soon emerged from the changing room, clearly showering wasn't his strong point. A large patch of his face was still covered in mud, although at least he was now recognisable, unlike the muddied mess that left the field of play earlier.

'Well done, son,' said Mum. 'Dad said you were getting better, but you've really surprised me today.' Dad would normally take Jack to football but he had to work today so it was a nice chance for Mum to get involved.

'Thanks,' he replied. 'I'm starving now though.'

'Come on Ethan!' called Mum. He was still playing with his friends but soon turned and ran over to the car.

'Great game Jack, where are you now in the league?' he asked as he caught his breath.

'Second, I think, not too sure,' replied Jack as he climbed into the passenger seat.

It wasn't long before the three of them arrived home. As they pulled in the drive, so did Dad, back from work early for a change. The boys were first through the door and as per usual straight onto the sofa in front of the television.

'Good game?' asked Dad in the kitchen.

'Yes,' she said, 'they won, 3-0 I think. Jack did really well. How was work?'

'Fine, just wanted to get things sorted before the holidays. Talking of work when is Abi on until?' he asked.

'Only until two I think, she should be back any second,' replied Mum.

At that moment the front door opened and in came Abi.

'Just on cue,' laughed Dad, with Mum chuckling alongside him.

Abi headed straight into the lounge and beckoned the two boys quietly upstairs. Mum and Dad were deep in conversation in the kitchen and seemed oblivious to the scheming of the children. Upstairs Abi talked through her plan with the boys. Her idea was for them to try and gather as much information about 'Christmas' from the locals in the village, the idea was to pretend they were doing a project at school looking into the old traditions and their focus was on 'Christmas'. The boys agreed that this was a good idea and that they would prepare some questionnaires to use. They didn't really want to question Mum and Dad too much as they could see they were uncomfortable speaking about it, so they figured it would be better to ask a few of the village folk some questions.

That evening they prepared their questionnaires upstairs. The plan was for the boys to work as a pair and Abi to work alone; they would canvas the village asking a few choice questions and try to get as many answers as possible. Mum and Dad were pleased of the peace and quiet that night and didn't question their motives. Abi was, as always, paying attention to detail and producing some creative and artistic worksheets, whereas Jack was far more matter of fact, creating basic questionnaires, ensuring that him and Ethan had their route planned and were trying not to miss out any houses in their sector.

CHAPTER 7
Investigation

SUNDAY, 15TH DECEMBER

The following morning the three of them got ready to begin their survey. Mum assumed they were going to the field as normal. They left the house together and headed down to the village square where Abi gave them their instructions.

'Right boys, have you got the list of streets and houses I've prepared?' she asked. 'Now let's head off and question who we can. Remember to stick to the questionnaire, it's important we're all asking the same questions.'

Jack wasn't too keen on his sister's plan, he wasn't much for questioning people. Ethan on the other hand was instinctively nosy and this was sure to be a huge help. Abi had decided that the boys would work as a pair and that she would go it alone. The three of them set off in their quest for information.

The villagers were very forthcoming with their answers that morning and the children were told many fond tales about Christmas. There didn't seem to be anyone who didn't enjoy Christmas and they all spoke about it in glowing terms.

Many of the stories were similar and talked about a magical, festive feeling among the villagers and how Christmas was a time for everyone to get together and to enjoy each other's company. However, each and every story was tainted with a great sadness, this was evident when they talked about how Christmas came to an end and how the awful accident up on the pass seemed to coincide. The accident was something the children knew little about and if they were honest they didn't care to. One thing that did catch their notice though was that several of the villagers felt there was something peculiar about the crash but they couldn't put their finger on it.

'The only good thing to come of out that awful incident was Kris,' said several of the villagers. They were referring to a local man known as 'Old Kris'. Apparently he had been travelling on the bus that fateful night and was badly injured, and these injuries had led to him losing his memory. The result was that he had stayed in the village ever since making it his home much to the delight of the locals who had grown very fond of him.

Abi had finished her route and was waiting for the other two near the library, she texted Jack to see where they were. Just as the message was sent they appeared, bundles of paper in their hands, not the neat pile that Abi had, but that was no surprise.

'All done?' she asked.

'Just one house to go,' replied Jack. 'Old Kris.'

'I'll come with you then, I may as well,' said Abi.

The three of them headed up the path behind the library to Old Kris' cottage. His home was very inviting, with soft lighting and several full-bodied trees in his front garden. The cottage itself was more like a log cabin in structure. The gate was decorated with some holly leaves and creaked loudly as Jack pushed it open. Ethan dashed up ahead of them and knocked on the large wooden door. After a few seconds the door opened and there stood Kris, a chubby old man with a huge white beard, dressed from head to toe in green. He was a real sight.

'Hello kids,' he said, 'what can I do for you?'

'We're doing a survey,' replied Abi. 'Can we ask you a few questions?'

'Sure, but come in, it's freezing out there,' said Kris.

They stepped inside to be greeted by a roaring log fire and the sweetest smell. Kris' home was delightful, cosy beyond belief and so welcoming.

'Cocoa anyone?' he asked.

'Yes please,' replied Ethan in a flash.

'What about you two?' asked Kris looking at Abi and Jack.

'That would be lovely,' replied Abi, answering for both of them.

Kris disappeared into the kitchen and the three of them sat down on the large sofa in front of the fire. They couldn't stop looking around, the house was so well presented, with objects hanging from everywhere, in particular two large wet socks hanging in front of the fire to dry. Jack pointed at them and sniggered.

Kris returned from the kitchen with three large mugs of cocoa and three small pies for the children. He then sat down to answer the questions the three had for him. One by one they asked their questions, but it soon became clear that Kris' injury had robbed him of his memories and he was unable to offer much insight into Christmas. Despite this setback the children continued to go through their questions methodically and Kris was happy to listen, even though he couldn't offer much help. They spent more time that day asking Kris questions than they did the rest of the village, in all honesty that was probably so that they could spend more time there drinking cocoa and enjoying his pies – a recipe that had survived Kris' accident much to the delight of the children.

After finally finishing their questions the children gathered their things and made for the door.

'Well, I wish I could have been more help,' said Kris.

'That's OK,' replied Abi laughing, 'your pies made up for it.'

'Well, anytime you want more, just come a knocking,' he replied. The look on Ethan's face indicated that he would hold him to his word.

The children said their goodbyes then made their way back down to the village square before heading home. When they arrived back home Mum was busy preparing tea, so she was happy to see the three of them back home. They rushed upstairs straight into Abi's room. Pulling the door shut behind them Abi pulled out her questionnaires and asked the boys to do likewise.

'Right, let's go through these and look for some sort of clues,' she said.

They were all aware that they needed to come up with a pair of five-letter codes or words to open the Advent Calendar that was stashed under Jack's bed.

'Let's make a list of any five letter words that we come across,' suggested Jack and that's exactly what they started to do,

Holly, elves, gifts – the list went on and on. In the meantime Jack had fetched the book from under his bed and it was sitting on Abi's bed. They had covered the top of the book just leaving the combination exposed. Jack was trying word after word, but nothing seemed to be working. Abi had finished going through her surveys and was also looking at the notes she had made that day in the library, but nothing was working.

'This is no good,' moaned Jack, 'nothing's working.'

'Only that Santa Claus guy knows,' said a resigned Ethan.

'Santa Claus!' replied Abi.

'Yes, that guy with the sled,' replied Jack.

'No, I mean Santa Claus,' said Abi. 'Try Santa Claus!'

Jack looked puzzled for a second, clearly not understanding what Abi meant, then it dawned on him and he pulled the partially covered book towards him and reached for the combination. His fingers were shaking as he turned the dials to spell out the words Santa Claus. The final 'S' clicked into place and the book suddenly went dim. All three heard a definite click. Jack removed the sweater from the top of the book and noticed the clasp had opened. He looked at both Abi and Ethan in turn before slowly opening the book.

CHAPTER 8
The Adventure Beckons

SUNDAY, 15TH DECEMBER

'What does it say, what does it say?' asked Ethan desperately.

Looking puzzled Jack replied, 'Nothing… Oh wait a minute, hang on.'

Jack had opened the book and was staring at a blank page surrounded with a scroll-like border, almost Celtic in appearance. Then very slowly text appeared on the page as if by magic.

By now the other two were standing over Jack and watching intently as the words appeared before them.

This is the property of Father Christmas and if found must be returned by those who found it as a matter of urgency.

You must beware as you will face a perilous journey to return the book, but millions of children across the world depend on its return.

Follow the instructions as they appear; the book will guide you. Tell no one of your discovery, the fate of Christmas lies with you.

'Oh my God, oh my God,' exclaimed Ethan. 'We must tell Mum and Dad.' He was full of excitement and Jack looked at Abi and shook his head.

'We can't tell anyone Eth, it says that quite clearly. Abs do you agree?' he asked.

Abi wasn't sure, but after a small pause she agreed. This book was evidently something out of the ordinary and they felt they had to trust the instructions they were being given. Jack's focus returned to the book and he turned the first page, again exposing blank pages but this time they waited for the instructions to appear and slowly the words formed on the paper:

Meet the Polar Express at 3am on December the 18th at the place shown on the map below, it will take you to Frozen Claw.

Sure enough a map appeared just below the instructions. It was a map of their home town and the surrounding area. It wasn't like any map they had seen before and it had an animated drawing of a train arriving at a marked point on the map.

Clearly this book had powers of its own and the three of them were being drawn in to the whole adventure. Would they really decide to take this adventure on without help? Abi who was usually the rational thinker was unusually quiet.

'What is it Abs?' asked Jack, he had noticed how his sister was for once lost for words.

'This just feels like a dream, it can't be what we think it is…can it?' she replied.

The children had only just started to learn about this 'Christmas' phenomenon and yet seemed to be embroiled in a huge undertaking. One thing the eldest two seemed to be forgetting was the time-scale and Ethan was quick to point this out.

'That's this Wednesday,' he yelped. 'Three days away, what are we going to do?'

'Calm down, we'll figure this out,' replied Jack. 'Just be quiet for a minute.'

Both Abi's and Jack's minds were working overtime trying to make sense of what had just happened and also considering how they could begin to consider completing this 'task'.

'Right!' exclaimed Abi. 'We're going to do this and we're going to do this right, so we can't tell anyone. We need to make plans but it's getting late now so let's go to bed and we'll start planning tomorrow.'

The boys seemed happy to follow Abi's lead and Jack packed the book away before they all headed off to bed. It was quite some time before they managed to get to sleep with all the various thoughts running through their heads, Abi's planning was well underway.

MONDAY, 16TH DECEMBER

Over the next few days the three of them collected supplies from the list Abi had compiled – iPhones, torches, batteries, coats, rucksacks, rope, Swiss army knife to mention just a few. Abi was nothing if not thorough and had covered virtually every eventuality. One of their biggest challenges was hoarding food.

Their Mum had noticed that a crazy amount of food was being consumed in the house, but was at least happy that the kids were eating well. Monday night's dinner was quite comical as Jack and Ethan tried to remove food from their dinner plates into Tupperware containers hidden beneath their clothing; several times Abi laughed out loud to the surprise of her parents.

'What's tickled you?' asked her mother.

'Oh …I'm just picturing Max knocking those boys over,' she quickly replied.

Her Dad had a little chuckle to himself, clearly that was an image that caused much amusement.

CHAPTER 9
The Journey Begins

TUESDAY, 17TH DECEMBER

The three of them all made the most of their chance to have a lie in as it was probably the last one they'd have for a few days at least. Mum was glad of the peace and quiet as she seemed to have plenty of chores to get done before they started making plans for their upcoming break. Abi spent the day checking and double-checking her 'supplies'; she was almost obsessive with her attention to detail. Jack spent the days casually watching classic films that were generally shown this time of year. Ethan on the other hand was doing everything in his power to keep the secret from Mum. He decided that the best plan was to spend as much time in his room, away from his mother, amusing himself with hours of gaming on his Xbox.

The night of their impending adventure came quickly upon the three of them and early into Wednesday morning they gathered in Abi's room. They were trying to be as quiet as possible as Abi was going through her checklist and making sure nothing was missing. She was impressed at how organised the boys had been and how much food they had managed to gather.

Ethan was overly keen for his rucksack to be handed back.

'Come on Abs let me get it on,' he said as Abi was finishing checking the pack.

'OK…what the…?' she said as she pulled out a small teddy bear from the bottom of his rucksack.

Jack chuckled as Ethan snatched the toy back from Abi.

'Woody has to come,' said Ethan in a demanding voice.

'Well, I suppose he can't cause much harm,' replied Abi handing over Ethan's rucksack to him.

The three of them crept across the landing and down the stairs into the kitchen where they were greeted by Max who was eager not to be left behind.

'Damn, Mum left him in the kitchen,' said Jack. 'He'll start barking like an idiot the minute we step out the back door.'

Max was very protective of the children and they all knew that if they left the house at night without him, he would undoubtedly create a fuss and wake their parents.

'We've got no choice said Abi, get his lead, he's going to have to come with us. Ethan you take hold of him.'

Taking Max wasn't ideal, but perhaps he'd come in handy and at least they could slip away quietly without waking their parents. Just as they were set to leave, Abi pulled out a small envelope and placed it on the kitchen worktop.

'What's that?' asked Jack.

'Just a little note for Mum, telling her not to worry,' replied Abi. 'Oh, hang on, I'll need to tell her about Max,' she added, scribbling something else onto the note before putting it back into the envelope.

In all honesty it was unlikely that a small note would put her Mum's mind at ease, but at least it might help a little thought Abi.

The three of them set off out the back door and down the path through the deserted village. Once they were through the village and on the outskirts they paused to take a look again at the map inside the Advent Calendar. It was even more spectacular outside as it glowed brightly in order to let them read the map.

'That lights up like my tablet,' giggled Ethan. The other two just looked at him a little impatiently. Jack was able to make sense of the map and appeared to know where they should be headed. They walked for quite some time to their destination, or at least what they thought was their destination. They had arrived at an old abandoned train station but there were no tracks… nothing.

'This can't be it,' said Abi looking pensively at Jack.

'Well, it's what the map says. This is definitely the spot, but we are a little early,' he replied.

'A little early,' she barked back. 'Looking at this place we're about a hundred years too late, there aren't even any tracks here, this is a waste of time.'

Jack was adamant that he had read the map correctly and pointed out over and over to Abi that they were still early. The early hours and the cold were making the three of them weary and Ethan sat down with Max listening to the other two bicker for quite some time when suddenly he said, 'Shut up you two… listen.'

They both looked at Ethan and then off into the distance as they could hear a faint humming sound. A distant light appeared and they all looked at each other excitedly. The humming slowly turned into a louder noise, the familiar sound of a train and as the light grew brighter they knew they were in the right spot.

'I told you, I told you!' yelled Jack, his voice almost being drowned out by the fast emerging train.

The three of them took a step back from where they were standing, unsure of where exactly the train would stop; with no tracks in sight they couldn't be sure.

The train itself was enormous and magnificent; it was an old steam train in impeccable condition. A huge grill stuck out at the bottom of the front of the train like some kind of snow plough, the headlight was huge and shone brightly. They looked back and could see at least four large carriages. There were steps up to the carriages but the ones in front of the children appeared to glow dimly. They were apprehensive and hesitant to step on board.

'Well, well, well,' boomed a voice. 'We haven't had passengers for many a year. Climb on board and enjoy the ride ladies and gentlemen,' said the train's ticket master who was standing at the top of the steps. He beckoned them all, Max included, onto the train.

Ethan and Max rushed up the steps quickly followed by Abi with Jack bringing up the rear. The carriage was really old fashioned with wooden seats padded with soft red cushions. They all quickly sat down and Ethan beckoned Max to sit up beside him. He placed his bag between himself and the window as a makeshift pillow.

The ticket master, dressed smartly in his uniform, headed towards them down the carriage.

'Do you have your tickets?' he asked as they got comfortable in their seats.

'Um…' Abi started to reply when Ethan nudged her tilting his head towards the Calendar. It had begun to glow and Abi opened it up; lo and behold four tickets were inside the front cover. She duly handed them over and the ticket master punched them and handed them back.

'Sit back and enjoy the ride,' he said as the train slowly pulled out of the station and began its journey.

Within just a few minutes the train was moving at a steady pace and the children looked out to their right and could see their village all lit up by the street lights and the occasional house light. The three of them looked at each other with an expression of almost disbelief. A few days ago they were just enjoying the school break and sledging with their friends, but now they were on some sort of mystical train, following a trail in an increasingly mystical book.

'I still can't believe we're doing this,' said Abi.

'I know, it's crazy,' replied Jack.

With that they both turned round to hear the grunt-like snore of Ethan, who was already fast asleep pressed up against his rucksack. The other two were far from sleep as the train seemed to glide effortlessly across the snowy terrain, they couldn't keep their eyes off the landscape.

It was difficult to see up ahead due to all the recent snowfall and the steam coming from the engine. Abi and Jack really struggled to make out any sort of track, it was as if the train was making its own way through the wilderness. They both looked at each other with a look of almost disbelief tinged with a hint of excitement. What was this quest they had stumbled upon?

CHAPTER 10
Panic

THURSDAY, 19TH DECEMBER

It was now almost six o'clock and back home Dad was starting to stir. He always got up pretty early and was generally off to work before the rest of them were awake. He went through his early morning routine as normal and as quietly as ever. The car was covered in snow on the drive and he started the engine before popping back inside for a cup of tea. The letter on the kitchen top somehow managed to escape his attention and he finished his drink before quietly leaving the house and heading off down the driveway. He only had a few more days before the holiday season and the family break which he had certainly earned this year. He backed off the drive and pulled away slowly, almost as if he was trying not to wake the neighbours.

Mum was still soundly asleep and it was only an hour or so before her alarm would wake her. Abi's letter would undoubtedly send her into a panic even though it was intended to do the opposite. The children had never done anything like this before but between them they felt they had the strength of conviction to complete this task they had been set.

Back on board the train it was now almost five hours into the journey. They had been passing through dense forest and rugged landscapes when they suddenly saw a break in the snow. Up ahead lay what looked like a lake, but it seemed to have a strange shimmer; as they drew closer it was obvious that the lake was frozen over.

'No way!' said Jack clearly confused as to how the train would cross the lake. It was surely too heavy and would break the ice.

'Hold on!' said Abi as the train entered the frozen lake. The moonlight was bouncing off the ice and creating a magical glow all around. The experience was like nothing they had ever seen before and most probably would never see again. The train seemed oblivious to the icy conditions and ploughed on across the lake without hesitation. It was quickly dawning on the pair that this was no ordinary journey and that unlike trains and tracks of their day, this train had almost a mind of its own and would let nothing get in its way.

Beep… beep…beep sounded Mum's alarm, alerting her to the fact that it was now 7.45 a.m. She reached over lethargically to hit the snooze button, before rolling back on her side to enjoy an extra ten minutes. Like every other morning, those ten minutes seemed to last just ten seconds before she was disturbed again by the alarm. This time she wearily climbed out of bed and made her way across the bedroom into the en suite for her morning shower.

'Up you get,' she shouted out of the bedroom door as a reminder to her children before she got into the shower. Whilst rinsing her hair she looked puzzled as she intently listened for a sound of the children stirring, but with no luck. She shook her head while grinning to herself at the prospect of them oversleeping.

'Come on Abi, you've got work in an hour,' she called out as she made her way downstairs. Still unaware of what was going on she headed into the kitchen to make breakfast. She put the kettle on and reached into the fridge for some milk.

'Are you having cereal or do you want some toast?' she shouted upstairs, but there was no reply.

'Abi?' she called again. There was no sign of a response, not a sound of beds creaking. Everything seemed a little too quiet so she headed upstairs to give Abi a little move on. She opened the bedroom door and was surprised to see the bed made and no Abi. She checked the bathroom and them went into the boys' rooms. Suddenly she was starting to feel a sense of panic. She ran downstairs and opened the back door calling out their names.

'Abi, Jack, Ethan?' she yelled. Back inside she headed straight for the phone. Dialling frantically she entered Abi's number; it took an age for the phone to finally ring, but it was a strange ring tone, slightly longer than usual, the kind you have when you are calling someone overseas. After several rings it went to answer phone and Abi's voicemail message came up. Initially she thought the strange ringtone meant that she must have dialled incorrectly, but this was Abi's message, how can this be right?

It was at that point she spotted the note that had been left on the kitchen table. She snatched at it quickly and opened it frantically. It read:

Mum,
First of all I don't want you to panic as we're not in trouble
and we're all together and OK. There's something important
that the three of us have to do and we'll be home as soon as
possible. You know I'm sensible and will take care of the
other two. I'm sorry I can't say anymore as I have to keep
what we're doing secret, but please don't worry Mum.
I love you and I'll text you later if I can.
Abi
P.S. Max is with us

The letter just fell to the floor as she felt physically sick with worry. Where were they? Where were they going? What were they doing? Question after question ran through her head and she started to panic.

She reached straight for her phone and tried Abi again but got the same response. She hung up and immediately dialled her husband Josh. He was stuck in traffic, still some way off his office.

'Hi darling, would you believe I'm still in on the road?' he said, oblivious to the situation back at home.

'Josh! Josh! The children, Abi…' she stuttered.

'Slow down, slow down,' he replied. 'What's going on?'

'They've gone, they've gone,' she added.

'What do you mean they've gone? Gone where?' clearly Josh was making no sense of his wife and decided to pull over so he could pay full attention to what she was saying.

'Hang on, I'll take you off hands free,' he said, picking up his mobile and switching off the hands free kit.

'Right go on,' he added.

'Abi's left me a note. The three of them have gone off somewhere. I've tried phoning her but something's wrong with her phone. I don't know what to do. I don't know what to do,' she repeated.

'OK, OK, try to keep calm,' he replied. 'I'll turn back now, the traffic the other way is clear, I'll be home in twenty-five minutes. Hold on,' he added as he started to turn the car round, almost clipping another car in his haste.

The journey back was much easier as the traffic at that time of day was generally heading into town. It didn't even take twenty minutes to get home, although to be fair Josh was driving rather quickly. His wife was waiting in the doorway as he pulled onto the drive.

'Shall I call the police?' she asked as he got out of the car.

'Just let me see the note first, let's not panic,' he replied. It wasn't easy for her not to panic, this was something so out of character for Abi and was not something they had ever had to deal with before.

After reading the letter Josh tried all three of the children's mobiles. The boy's phones were switched off and Abi's was still ringing with the same strange ring tone.

'Right, I'll call Mike,' said Josh. Mike was the town's local policeman and was a good friend of Josh's. It took only a minute or so for him to get hold of Mike and he agreed to come over as soon as possible. It was now nine o'clock and unknown to Mum and Dad the children had been gone for over seven hours and were in fact six hours into their train journey. Mum was upstairs searching through their rooms looking for any clues as to where they may have gone.

'Found anything?' Dad asked as he popped his head round the corner into Abi's room.

'Nothing that makes sense,' she barked back. 'Sorry,' she added, 'I didn't mean to snap.'

'That's OK,' he said giving her a reassuring hug as they sat down on the edge of Abi's bed.

Her computer and desk were all covered with Christmas information and some articles on the crash all those years ago.

'Looks like she's been finding out about Christmas,' said Dad. 'I wish they'd had a chance to enjoy Christmas like we did, maybe one day.'

Mum started crying at this point, she clearly was in a real mess about the situation and felt so powerless. Just then there was a knock at the door and a voice called out.

'Josh, Gwen, you there?'

It was Mike, he'd come round as quickly as he could to help out.

'Right, take me through everything you know,' he asked.

Mum and Dad told Mike what little they knew. They explained how they had searched for clues, tried their mobiles and also showed Mike the letter. Mike was at a loss just like the worried parents.

'Well, I think the first thing we should do is start contacting any friends or even knock on a few doors to see if anyone has seen or heard anything. I'll call the station and see if we can get some help,' he suggested.

Mum and Dad seemed in total agreement, after all Mike was the expert so they had to trust his judgement. They both picked up their mobiles and grabbed their coats, ready to get out into the village and start calling people.

'Hold on,' said Mike. 'One of you needs to stay here in case they call or come back,' he added. Mum was the obvious choice as she was in no state to go knocking on doors and speaking to people.

'We'll keep you up to date,' said Dad as he and Mike headed out to start looking.

The next few hours flew by, Dad and Mike were busy knocking on doors, speaking to the locals with another officer who had joined in to help the search. Mum was busy phoning everyone and anyone but with no success. She had also tried Abi's phone now twenty times but with no joy. With every minute that went by Mum was getting more and more worried, her only hope lay in the fact that the three were together, or at least that's what she hoped. Not one of their neighbours could offer any insight into the children's disappearance, but most of them commented on how they had all seen the children last Sunday as they carried out their 'Christmas survey'.

Back on board the train the children had just reached the end of the frozen lake and the train was now heading up a narrow pass in the mountains. It was a steady climb to the top. The gradient of the path was beyond any normal train's capabilities and in all honesty that of most motor vehicles. Abi wasn't a huge fan of heights and she was doing her best not to look out of the window as the train wound its way up the mountain.

The climb seemed never ending and the afternoon light was fading fast. The train finally approached the summit just as the last of the daylight disappeared. Fighting her fear of heights Abi mustered the strength to look out of the window to her left. The lake they had spent several hours crossing now looked so small below them, but at the same time it looked majestic as the light of the full moon lit it up like a huge dance floor. She was transfixed on the lake until Jack disrupted her thoughts.

'The aurora, the aurora!' he yelped as the train reached the summit. 'I've always wanted to see it,' he added.

In the distance he and Ethan, who had only just woken up, could see the wave-like image glowing bright green. What a sight it made, it surpassed even Jack's wildest expectations. It was one of those moments that they would remember all their lives and one of the world's great wonders. Many people travelled from far afield to see this sight and now it was clear why. It was magical in appearance and almost other- worldly. Something though wasn't sitting right with Jack.

'But?' said Jack giving Abi a puzzled look. 'We're not supposed to see them from here, I thought we needed to be much further north?'

'Then where are we?' questioned Abi.

Jack reached down for the book that Max was sprawled across. He opened it and the map they had followed to the station had changed, it now showed a much larger area and a trail that was clearly the one they were travelling on. According to the map they were now hundreds of miles north and still going.

'This can't be right?' said a confused Jack.

'We just can't be? We haven't been travelling that long have we?' he added.

'I don't know what to think anymore,' replied Abi as she pulled out her mobile checking for a signal. She was desperate to send her Mum a text as she knew she would be crippled with worry. She had written the text and tried to send it sometime ago but as yet no signal had been available, so it was still stuck in her outbox.

This whole saga was proving as unpredictable as the British weather and nothing seemed impossible. The two of them tried to make sense of the map for a little while. Abi's geography skills were a little better than Jack's and between them they were starting to make sense of their location. The train must have been travelling at a much greater speed than they had realised, as they were hundreds of miles further north than they should be. They were, of course, still unaware of where their exact destination was.

'There's still no sign on this map as to where we are heading,' said Abi.

'I know. There aren't even any towns or cities anywhere near this point on the map,' Jack said as he looked at the map that appeared to show them they were travelling through an uninhabited area of Scandinavia.

'Where's that then?' piped up a now fully awake Ethan, pointing out of the window.

In the distance was a small cluster of lights that was growing closer by the minute. It soon became clear that it was a town. It looked pretty isolated as there were no other lights for miles around. Jack looked once again at the Calendar. A circle on the map now showed their impending destination; the name slowly started to appear. Just then the ticket master interrupted them.

'Next stop up ahead,' he called popping his head out of his office door. No sooner had he made his announcement than the name of the town appeared on the map, the ticket master, however, wasn't finished.

'Welcome to Frozen Claw,' he added.

CHAPTER 11
Frozen Claw

THURSDAY, 19TH DECEMBER

Policeman Mike was sitting in the lounge deep in conversation with a technician who was working vigorously on a laptop. Mum and Dad were standing in the kitchen talking to several friends who had all come round to offer help.

Just at that second Mum's mobile buzzed; quick as a flash she rushed to pick it up.

'It's Abi, it's Abi!' she screamed.

'Answer it quickly,' said Dad.

'It's a text, not a call,' she replied opening the message.

'Well?' asked Dad impatiently.

'Hang on, hang on,' she said. 'It says:

Hi mum, we're OK, don't worry, I'll keep them safe. 😊

She looked up puzzled.

'Is that it?' asked Dad.

'That's it,' she concluded.

Dad rushed through to the lounge to see how Mike was getting on with the technician. He had arrived to put some form of track on Abi's sim card, this would hopefully use the GPS on the phone to track their location. Mike was hopeful this new message would send a clear signal as to their position.

'Well?' asked Mike, looking at the technician who had a very puzzled look on his face.

'This can't be right, something must be confusing the system, perhaps it's the weather,' he replied as he turned the screen to show Mike the result of their GPS track.

'Damn, hopefully she'll text again soon,' Mike said as he looked at the screen that suggested the kids were way north of the UK, deep in the ice fields of Scandinavia. To Mike, the technician, and indeed the parents, this was impossible. They didn't even contemplate that the children could be where the GPS suggested.

'Well, at least she's made contact,' Dad responded. 'She sounds OK. She's a sensible girl, we've just got to have faith,' he added, putting his arm around his wife.

Back in Frozen Claw the train pulled away from the station as imperiously as it had arrived back in Willow Cove. The children stood on the station looking down the frozen high street. They were conscious that the book was starting to glow and, wanting to keep it out of sight of prying eyes, Jack and Abi told Ethan to keep a lookout as they stepped behind the station building to see what the next message was. Ethan was standing alongside Max. He was totally transfixed by the sight of the town, it was a little like an old Wild West town, but frozen and covered in snow. There were lights on in most of the buildings and a lot of noise coming from the far end of the high street. Multi-coloured lights were littered along the side of the street, hanging from ropes strewn between the buildings.

Behind the station Jack and Abi opened the book that slowly, right on cue, revealed a new message:

Go to the Broken Sled Tavern, speak to Tiberius and ask him to take you to Claw Cavern. You need to find Fang.

The opposite page was fully animated, showing a town decorated magnificently, with people dancing in the street, houses lit up with their doors open and loads of people coming and going. A real Christmas town like the children had learnt about during their brief investigations. The animation bore no resemblance to the town they were in. There were no decorations, there were no people singing, just the occasional howl of a distant wolf, abandoned and damaged sleds scattered down the sides of the street.

'Do you think this is the same place?' asked Jack.

'I guess so,' replied Abi. 'But what happened?'

They were both unsure as to why things had gone so wrong in this town, but knew they had to stay on track. They put the Calendar away in Jack's backpack and collected Ethan and Max before making their way down the street. They were drawn to the noise at the far end of the high street. As they walked down the street they were passed by the odd stranger, everyone was heavily wrapped up due to the cold and seemed very unwelcoming and distant.

The place at the end of the street was a noisy tavern full of rowdy people, not the sort of place the children were at all used to. The tavern had a broken sign hanging down to the left of the main door and Jack tilted his head to read what it said.

'This is it, this is The Broken Sled,' he said pointing to the sign.

Ethan looked petrified, this was the last place he wanted to be, but he had no choice as they had to stick together. Clearly this tavern was no place for dogs so Abi quickly tied Max to the rail outside. With Jack in front, they stepped up onto the decking outside the front of the tavern and headed inside.

The tavern was poorly lit inside, thick with smoke and the clientele weren't of the highest standard. Lots of old, bearded men who clearly spent too much time in the establishment. They looked around anxiously for somewhere to sit. There were a few spaces in the corner next to a man dressed in a long, dark, winter coat, who had his nose buried in a book.

'Over there,' pointed Jack to the small space. Abi ushered Ethan in front of her and they made their way between the patrons in the crowded bar and sat down at the vacant table.

Jack followed, but as the two sat down he turned and looked over towards the bar.

'Where are you going?' she asked Jack.

'To ask for Tiberius,' he responded, before turning around and heading over to the bar.

It wasn't easy to get to the bar, there were people queuing to be served and Jack wasn't confident enough to nudge his way through, so he waited patiently. He was getting the odd strange look here and there, clearly he was out of place, but in a room full of some of the strangest characters he had ever seen, he wasn't overly worried about standing out.

He finally made his way to the front, only to be greeted by an overly aggressive barman.

'What can I get you?' he boomed.

'Nothing…er… I mean I just need some help,' replied Jack nervously.

'I serve drinks here, it's not the information service,' he said sarcastically, laughing with some of his regulars at the bar.

'I'm just looking for someone,' Jack quickly added.

'Aren't we all,' replied the barman, clearly fancying himself as a part-time comedian.

'It's Tiberius,' said Jack.

Suddenly the noise seemed to dim a little and the barman looked confused.

'That's a name I haven't heard for a long time,' he said. 'Not seen him in years.'

Jack's face dropped, this wasn't the answer he needed. What now? He turned and headed back over to his brother and sister.

Over on the far side of the tavern, Jack appeared to have drawn the attention of two men who were whispering to each other and looking over at the three children.

Jack stood in front of his siblings and gave them the bad news.

'He's not here,' he said,

'What do you mean he's not here?' replied Abi.

'Exactly that, he's not here,' he said again.

'What about Fang?' piped up Ethan. Just at that point the man who had been sitting next to them stood up and brushed by them as he made his way out of the tavern.

'Ssshh,' said Jack to Ethan. 'We don't know who's supposed to hear that name, we need to be careful,' he warned.

'Now what?' he added looking at Abi.

Abi sat pensively, trying to plan their next move.

Just at that point the door of the tavern opened and the cold wind from outside blew into the bar. A man dressed in a long trench coat and a black hat stood at the threshold. Silence fell over the bar, all eyes turned initially to him and then everyone turned away, seemingly desperate to avoid eye contact. He walked slowly towards the bar accompanied by a huge black hound. He was scouring the room as he walked. He whispered something to the barman who looked panicky as he shook his head and took a step back. Clearly he was not able to help the man and obviously felt threatened by his presence.

The man looked around the room once more, then he caught Abi's stare. He headed across towards the children. Suddenly another man ran into the bar and called out, 'Mr Grimm!'

With that the approaching man stopped and turned to see who was calling his name.

The man at the door added, 'Mr Grimm, you'd better come.' The man turned around to take another look at Abi before heading out of the tavern with his hound.

'Who was that and why was he looking at you?' asked Ethan, clearly aware that neither of his siblings would have any more of a clue that he did.

Abi looked visibly shaken, 'Let's not wait to find out,' she said.

'Well, we need to find somewhere to stay. Let's go and see what we can find,' she added. They seemed to have reached a dead end but they needed somewhere to sleep for the night. They would start their enquiries again in the morning and hopefully they would get a better response. Abi made the decision to lead the other two out of the tavern and back into the high street looking down the street for a sign of a hotel or guesthouse.

They stepped down from the entrance to the tavern and out onto the street.

Just at that moment Jack felt a hand on his shoulder, he turned worriedly.

'Quickly, follow me,' said the man who had been sitting next to them in the pub reading his book.

Almost instinctively the three of them decided to follow his instructions. This wasn't their usual reaction to dealing with a stranger but somehow without thinking they followed him. He led them a few doors down the high street, before turning down a side alley between two run-down properties.

The night air was bitterly cold and the high street was almost deserted, but Jack felt like they were being watched. As they turned down the alley he looked back over his shoulder to see the two men from the tavern standing outside the front door looking in their direction. He didn't want to worry the other two so, although he was feeling a little uncomfortable, he decided not to burden them with his anxiety.

About twenty yards or so down the alley they reached a dimly lit guest house and the man led them inside.

'Wait here while I find a room,' he said quietly as they stood in what appeared to be the hall of the property. Then he disappeared through another door. Clearly he knew someone at the guest house, or so they assumed. He returned in a matter of seconds clutching what looked like a room key in one of his hands.

'I've got you a room for the night,' he said handing the key to Abi, 'but before you head up let's get a quick drink.'

The three children seemed to be in a bit of a trance, they didn't question the man once and seemed content to follow his instructions. He had a confident air and at the same time gentle demeanour about him and this had put the children at ease the second they had come into contact with him.

'Come through,' he said opening the door to a room which was some kind of bar for residents of the guest house. No one was in there and he told them to sit down around a table.

'So what do you want with Tiberius?' he asked.

'How did you know we were looking for Tiberius?' Abbey quickly replied.

'I couldn't help but overhear the young man at the bar,' he said tilting his head in Jack's direction.

'We can't really say,' said Abi. 'We have a message for him.'

'Well, I guess any message you have for me, I'd better hear,' he said with a cheeky grin.

The three children looked at each other inquisitively. Were they just to take his word for it? Could they trust him?

'How do we know you are Tiberius?' Ethan piped up from nowhere. This was almost the first thing he'd said since arriving at Frozen Claw. He'd been in such awe of everything and everyone that they had encountered along their journey, he'd been walking around in some form of magical daydream. But were their plans starting to fall apart and was this journey about to become a nightmare?

'Good point,' replied Tiberius clearly thinking of how he could solve this predicament. Then he seemed to remember something and reached inside his long dark coat. He pulled out what appeared to be some sort of old medal, it was quite dirty, but as he rubbed it down the front of his coat the children started to see the object was indeed some kind of star-shaped badge. He handed it to Abi. Upon closer inspection she could see two words on the badge 'Sheriff...Tiberius'.

Although the badge was old and worn there was no doubt that it belonged to Tiberius and that in all likelihood this man was indeed Tiberius.

'But why did the barman say he hadn't seen you in years?' asked a suspicious Jack.

Tiberius paused for thought before he responded.

'It's been quite some time since I helped to run this town. I've kept a pretty low profile for a long time now, I've kept myself to myself,' he said.

The children weren't sure what to do, but if this was not Tiberius they had reached a dead end so they had to take a risk. Abi looked at Jack as she handed him the badge, he looked up and nodded at Abi.

'OK, we have message for you. Well, a kind of a request I suppose,' she said.

'I see,' said Tiberius as he waited for more information.

Jack placed his backpack on the table and reached in to pull out the Calendar. As he removed it he could see Tiberius start to shift slightly in his seat; they now had his full attention.

'Where did you get that?' he asked.

'Back home,' replied Jack, 'back in Willow Cove.'

'Where?' asked Tiberius.

Jack turned the book around to show Tiberius the page that was mapping their journey to date. The start of the journey was clearly marked and the substantial distance they had already covered was clear.

'But how did you get here?' he added.

'The Calendar,' said Abi. 'We've followed the instructions and that's what led us to you.' Abi continued by telling Tiberius about the discovery of the Calendar and their decision to follow the instructions to the letter. From leaving their hometown to travelling on board the Polar Express. Abi made him aware of their sacrifice and how they were unable to share their adventure with their parents who would clearly be out of their minds with worry.

Tiberius rocked back in his chair, clearly surprised as to what he had just heard. He found it astonishing that the children had shown such commitment to this quest.

'Well, I'm impressed,' he said, watching Jack turn the Calendar back around. Abi then proceeded to turn to the relevant page. Again the message was clear:

Go to the Broken Sled Tavern, speak to Tiberius and ask him to take you to Claw Cavern. You need to find Fang.

Ethan couldn't keep his eyes off the animated pages that showed Frozen Claw in a totally different light, warm and welcoming and a place of such happiness.

'When was this?' he asked Tiberius, pointing at the images.

'Quite some time ago now,' he replied. 'Back when things were very different, before Lupus Grimm ran the town.'

'Who?' asked Jack.

Tiberius went on to describe Lupus Grimm, a really nasty piece of work. Along with his henchmen he had managed to turn this once joyful town into a miserable and dark place. This had taken place quite some time ago and the locals now lived in constant fear of Lupus. The reason for the change wasn't exactly clear, but could their quest have some bearing on it? The children clearly understood the affect Lupus Grimm had on the town, even in the short time they had been there they had already witnessed his unnerving ability to intimidate.

'Is this how Christmas used to be?' said Ethan, still looking for more information.

'Yes, indeed young man,' replied Tiberius. 'Christmas was a wonderful time. But things do just come to an end sometimes, not many things go on forever.'

'Santa was the one guy who had the strength and courage to put Lupus in his place, he'd be sad to see this town now, but I guess he couldn't go on forever,' he said with a sense of sadness in his voice. Clearly Tiberius had seen much happier times in Frozen Claw and was emotional when he reminisced. It reminded Abi in particular of their parents when they discussed the topic of Christmas.

The three children had heard many tales of Christmas and how wonderful it used to be and even after travelling many hours to a foreign land those same stories were still being told. They all felt sad and disappointed that they had never had the chance to witness this magical festival.

'Anyway you three,' said Tiberius, 'I suggest you get a bite to eat and then a good night's sleep, we've got quite a journey ahead tomorrow.' The children were delighted that he had decided to help them. Their faces lit up and Tiberius could see he had made the right decision.

'In the morning I'll meet you across the street, there is a small deserted store, that's where I keep my sled,' he informed the children.

Ethan liked the sound of that, his ears pricked up instantly.

'A sled?' he asked.

'Yes, young man, that's how we travel round here,' chuckled Tiberius.

'Meet me over there at 6 a.m. sharp, we need to head off before first light,' he said. He bade the three of them goodnight and made his way out of the guest house. They headed up to bed, still a little bit confused as they had yet to see the owner of the guest house, but that was hardly the strangest thing they had encountered in the last few days.

All of a sudden Ethan yelped, 'Max!' The poor dog had been totally forgotten in their adventure, he was still tied up to the rail outside the Broken Sled.

'Oh my God!' responded Abi. 'Quick,' she added looking at Jack. Jack was already one step ahead of them and flew down the stairs and ran up the alley and across the street to find a petrified Max cowering behind a post at the end of the rail outside the tavern.

'Sorry boy,' said Jack giving his faithful companion a big hug. He then led Max back across the street and into the guest house. In his haste Jack had failed to notice that he was being watched. The two men from the tavern had now been joined by a third person. They could see across to where the children were staying and saw a faint glow coming from the room which was holding their gaze.

Back inside the guest house, Ethan was under his bed sheet eating cookies while looking at the Calendar and the amazing scene inside. He had not counted for the strength of the Calendar's glow and how it was gathering unwanted attention.

The night was still young, but after such an early start and with all the excitement of the journey the three were soon fast asleep. Before dropping off Abi had remembered their loved ones back home and sent another reassuring, or at least what she thought was a reassuring, text.

Just found somewhere safe to sleep for the night. We're all well and comfortable, please don't worry. ☺

Mum and Dad had been in full panic mode for quite some time now, and although the texts weren't exactly to their liking, they were at least evidence that the children were still, or at least they hoped, OK. They did not sleep as soundly as their children that night.

CHAPTER 12
A Threat to the Quest?

Abi was the first to wake. She looked at her watch and it was just past five o'clock. She leant across to Jack's bed and gave him a nudge.

'Eh… what… who?' mumbled Jack as he started to stir. Even though it was early they had actually managed to get quite a long night's sleep. This though didn't help Ethan's notoriously slow start. He was like a zombie first thing in the morning, so Abi knew they would have to get up with plenty of time to spare.

Unbeknown to the children, one of the three men who had been watching from across the street had stayed there all night, as what appeared to be some sort of lookout. Whilst his intentions were not known, had they been aware of his presence the children probably would not have slept so soundly.

After finally managing to get Ethan dressed, Jack packed away the last of their things. Abi completed her sixth check of the room to ensure nothing was left behind.

'Have you messaged Mum and Dad?' Jack asked Abi.

'Just a couple of times,' she replied. 'They'll be out of their minds with worry.'

'I think I'll send something,' suggested Jack, reaching into his rucksack to pull out his smartphone as he sat on the end of one of the beds.

The message he sent was short and to the point, but unknown to Jack would have a real bearing on the search efforts back home.

Back home the message reached Mum's mobile. Even though it felt like the middle of the night she was quick to respond to the text alert message on her phone. Dad had managed to get some sleep but was woken by his wife.

'Josh, Josh, it's from Jack's phone,' she said excitedly. They both ran downstairs where Mike was in the kitchen making himself a cup of coffee.

He looked like he'd been up all night and was pumping himself full of coffee to keep himself awake. They were eternally grateful to their friends for rallying and Dad put his arm around Mike's shoulders in a clear sign of his appreciation.

'It's from Jack,' said Mum handing the phone to Mike.

'Hang on,' he replied as he hurried into the lounge. He sat on the sofa next to the technician who was strangely wide awake showing no sign of tiredness. They looked at the data on the screen and looked at the text message again. They talked quietly between themselves with the technician shrugging his shoulders.

'What is it Mike?' said Dad.

'Well, it's a strange one, Josh, Abi and Jack are on two different networks and have sent messages at different times, but both signals are suggesting that the messages are coming from the same place,' he said. 'We thought Abi's signal GPS was being sent in error, but now with Jack's as well I can't see how this can be wrong.' They were starting to suspect that indeed the children had travelled some distance and needed to point their enquiries in that direction.

'Let's not panic, we've had a couple of messages now that seem they are from the kids and they don't sound like they are in any trouble. Let me make some calls and check out this GPS signal,' he said picking up his mobile and returning to the kitchen.

Mum and Dad were exhausted and as Mum slumped into the sofa, Dad returned to the kitchen to make them both a cup of tea.

Back in Frozen Claw the three children, along with Max, were leaving the guest house. They headed downstairs and out into the alley. Their breath was almost taken away by the biting cold. Ethan's face was a picture, almost as if someone had poured a cup of cold water down his back.

It was still very dark, although the moonlight and the pure white snow that lay all around gave the town an almost artificial light. They headed up the alley and started to make their way across the street. At that point they saw a man running quickly in the other direction.

'Who was that?' asked Abi, looking at her two brothers. Both shrugged their shoulders clearly unaware of who he was or why he was running. They approached the store that Tiberius had described and Abi knocked gently on the door. After a short wait the door opened slowly and Tiberius beckoned the three in before popping his head outside for a quick look around.

'Did anyone see you?' he asked.

'Don't think so,' replied Jack, 'although…'

'Although what?' asked Tiberius hurriedly.

'Well, there was a guy who seemed to run off when he saw us,' added Abi.

'Damn! We'd best get moving,' said Tiberius, clearly unnerved by what the children had told him.

He removed a huge tarpaulin from the far side of the room and underneath was a large sledge with eight strong-looking huskies just lying peacefully on the floor.

'Wow,' said Ethan as he moved towards the sledge, stroking it gently as if it were some sort of pet. It was a sturdy looking carriage, bigger than the average husky sled with storage pockets here and there and a large seating area, quite comfortable looking in fact.

'Up boys,' said Tiberius. With no further instruction the huskies stood up, starting to become almost restless with the urge to run. Max didn't look happy, these dogs looked quite intimidating. Or perhaps it was the thought of him having to join in and pull this mighty sled.

Down the far end of the street a group of men had started to make their way towards the store led by an aggressive looking man in a long leather coat, exactly like the man Tiberius had described. Indeed Lupus Grimm was heading in their direction. Tiberius had one last look out of the store and when he spotted the group he urged the children and Max to board the sled. Max took up his position alongside the huskies, was this really his place? He had no harness and in all honesty he had no clue! Tiberius unbolted both doors before climbing aboard his vehicle and taking the reins. The children all sat on board and held on tight. Ethan looked like a boy waiting at the start of a roller coaster, eyes wide and knuckles that had turned white from gripping too tightly.

'Mush, mush,' Tiberius said loudly as the men approached the store.

'Mush,' he called out again and with that the huskies leapt into action almost pulling the sledge clean through the air and out of the front of the store. The doors flew back knocking two of the approaching men clean off their feet. The dogs turned sharply left, the sled and its passengers skidded sideways across the street until the reins were pulled taught. They headed off past the tavern and out of the town.

The children could hear the men yelling in the distance and couldn't quite understand why they were yelling or in fact why they were in the street at such an early hour.

'What was all that about?' asked Jack.

'Who knows,' replied Tiberius. 'But they're not the kind of men we need to stop and chat with,' he added. Clearly Tiberius knew who it was that had come to intercept them that morning, but he decided that the children did not need the additional worry of such information.

Ethan was frantically looking all around the sledge clearly very agitated. 'Where's Max?' he asked close to panic. There was no sign of him among the huskies and Ethan feared he'd been left behind in the rush to get away. Abi and Jack too began to search for signs of their beloved pet. Just at that point a head popped out of one of the luggage spaces on the side of the sledge, perfect comedy timing as always from Max. He was clearly intimidated by the challenge of the huskies and he had dived into the luggage compartment just before they burst onto the street.

'Max, you're a loon,' said Ethan as the three of them laughed, clearly relieved to find their pet and friend on board.

CHAPTER 13
The Frozen North

Within no time at all the town was barely more than a faint glow in the distance. The huskies were relentless, they had hardly broken stride for the last hour and were making light work of the snowy conditions underfoot. The landscape was like something from a fairy tale, pure and white, with only the occasional spruce tree blotting the scene.

It was difficult for the children to understand how Tiberius could navigate in this terrain, there was hardly any point for reference and certainly no route or path to follow. Tiberius, however, was undeterred, this was his domain and he knew every drift and glacier almost by name.

'Is it far?' asked Jack, like any other back seat teenager.

'Further than you'd think,' replied Tiberius, 'but we should be there by nightfall.'

Abi looked gobsmacked, 'Nightfall?' she said, 'but that's hours, can the dogs keep up this pace?'

'Don't worry about them they'll do their bit, anyway we'll stop for a rest a little later on,' he replied.

The sled was travelling at quite some speed and Max's face and ears were flapping about comically. Ethan was trying to reach over to stroke his pet when he slipped head first towards the ground, he was only rescued by Tiberius' quick thinking as he reached across grabbing Ethan by the belt before placing him back into his seat.

'Steady young man,' he said. 'We can't have you falling into the snow and getting wet, that could be very dangerous out here,' he warned.

An embarrassed and slightly scared Ethan sat back down and huddled up under his fur blanket.

It occurred to Abi that they were heading on this mystery journey across some very harsh terrain to meet someone called Fang, who they knew nothing about and knew nothing of his intentions. Where had her common sense gone? Why was she so willing to head off into the unknown? This whole episode was really bringing out another side to her character, she wasn't sure what to think.

'Tiberius?' she asked

'Yes, what is it?' he replied.

'Who is Fang?' she asked. 'And how will he be able help us?'

There was a long pause, before Tiberius answered.

'Fang is a character that not many people have met, but if the Calendar is right, you need his help,' he said.

'Have you met him?' asked Abi.

'Our paths have crossed just a few times,' he replied, 'but not for many years now.'

His answer didn't really tell Abi anything, but she felt that she shouldn't probe too much more. Throughout their journey the three of them had sensed an underlying feeling of sadness and almost bitterness in the people they had encountered. The inhabitants of Frozen Claw were not exactly welcoming and even Tiberius had been quite dark and mysterious since they met him. They could only hope that this journey led to some happy conclusion and that they weren't wasting their time.

It was a couple of hours before Tiberius decided to rest the dogs and let the children stretch their legs.

'We'll stop here for an hour or so, just to let the dogs rest up,' he said after pulling over by a small cluster of spruce trees. The trees had a covering of snow on their peaks and provided a canopy for the children to walk around underneath as they explored the tiny forest.

Ethan had helped Max out of the sled and was playing with him as the other two talked with Tiberius.

Suddenly Max's ears pricked up as he stared into the distance.

'What is it mate?' asked Ethan as he watched Max study the horizon. Just at that moment Ethan saw a flicker of light, like a reflection from a piece of glass or metal. In this land of white on white Ethan dismissed it as commonplace and thought no more of it. Max was not so convinced and he had to be dragged back to the others by Ethan.

'What's up with him?' asked Jack.

'Just some silly reflection off in the distance,' Ethan replied.

Tiberius turned to look in the direction Ethan had pointed to. He looked studiously for five or more minutes.

Abi looked at Jack with a confused expression on her face. They couldn't understand what Tiberius was looking for and noticed he definitely appeared worried. Clearly Tiberius' mind was on the men they had left back in the town, were they following? Surely not.

'Perhaps we'll just give the dogs forty-five minutes,' he suggested as his gaze broke. He didn't want to take any unnecessary risks. It was his job to make sure the children were delivered to Fang safe and sound.

It wasn't long before they were back underway. The second part of the journey was much harder work for the poor dogs and after just an hour or so they were at the foot of a large mountain. They started to climb a gentle path which, from what the children could see, wound around to the left of the mountain. It was very hard in the daylight to make out much in the way of paths and routes due to the unyielding brightness, but as the afternoon light darkened slightly it was becoming easier to read the terrain.

After what seemed just a short time they had climbed about a third of the way up the mountain and had an amazing view of the landscape they had left below. Tiberius pulled hard on the reins instructing the dogs to stop. Out from a compartment in the sled he pulled an old fashioned telescope, an old brass model, like something from long ago. He snapped it open and used it to peer off into the distance below.

What he saw was not something he would share with the children. Lupus Grimm was on their trail, but he wasn't closing and could have no idea on their destination, or could he?

'What is it?' asked Jack worriedly.

'Er…nothing,' lied Tiberius. 'I'm just checking that our route is correct,' he added unconvincingly as he put his telescope away and ushered the dogs onwards. It was only another half hour or so when they came upon a small clearing. On the other side the path continued, but as they entered the clearing the dogs stopped. They jostled restlessly, whining slightly and growling at the same time.

'Calm boys, calm,' said Tiberius trying to reassure them.

'What's the matter?' asked Abi.

'This is where my part in your journey must end,' replied Tiberius. 'The dogs won't cross this clearing.'

'But why?' asked Jack.

'This isn't their domain,' he answered, 'but don't worry you've only got a mile or so to walk, the path is quite gentle and will lead you to Fang.'

'A mile!' screeched Ethan, 'but that's...' he stuttered, trying to finish his sentence. Maths was one of his strong points so when he finally worked out how far a mile was he calmed down, he had just had a bit of a brain freeze and panicked when he heard Tiberius speak.

Tiberius wanted the children to hurry so he could head off in another direction and hopefully put Lupus Grimm off their trail.

'Quick as you can, I need to get the boys back,' he said, trying to hurry the children without worrying them.

They quickly gathered their stuff together and said their goodbyes before heading off on foot across the clearing. Quick as a flash Tiberius was off, working the dogs hard to try and get away from the path as soon as possible.

'Do you think that was a bit odd Abs?' asked Jack.

'Isn't everything on this crazy adventure?' laughed Abi nervously.

The weather was now the children's enemy, even though they only had a short walk the temperature was incredibly low and dropping. They were fortunate they had packed their sledging kit which included plenty of base layers and snowboarding jackets.

The path on the other side of the clearing was pretty easy underfoot and had just a gradual climb, so presented no problem for the children. As they were walking they heard a piercing howl. Max quickly scurried between the children as they stopped to listen. The howl turned into two and then three and then many more. Max was clearly as unsettled as the children, he was almost circling the group as they continued their way up the path. Jack and Abi looked at each other with a worried look on their faces, they were just three average children stuck out in the wilderness on a very un-average adventure.

'Are there wolves out here?' asked Ethan.

'I've no idea,' replied Abi. 'Let's not hang around to find out,' she added as they picked up their pace. Unfortunately there were indeed wolves in the area and the children were very exposed as they followed the path through the snow. Jack heard a rustle in the trees below the path to the left, he ignored it and encouraged the other two to hurry up. Abi then saw something moving in the distance further up the path, she stopped suddenly, holding out a hand for Ethan and then the other for Jack. The three of them made a makeshift circle, with Max sheltering in the middle.

They were in trouble; a large silvery grey wolf started to climb slowly up the bank below to their left, another was slowly edging down the path towards them, snarling and showing its teeth, two more were above them on the mountainside. What could they do? They had watched nature show after nature show, they knew their best bet was to stand their ground and certainly not to run.

The number of wolves grew and they were closing in slowly on the three children who were clearly out of their depth. Amazingly there were no tears amongst the group, perhaps they had no time to think. They were more in shock than anything else, the only noise was coming out of Max who was trying to growl, but it was coming across as more of a whimper.

The wolves were now within ten metres and were slowly closing in. Their eyes were a piercing black, almost soulless and their long, pointy snouts were dribbling with drool, clearly ready to dine. Suddenly some of the wolves stopped growling and started to sniff the air, their expressions suddenly changing. They looked panicked as a strange groan of sorts sounded further up the path. The wolves looked at each other before turning to face up the path. They had lost interest in the children and were more concerned with the approaching noise. Within a matter of seconds the children's fate had changed as the wolves scattered quickly, running nervously in every direction until they finally disappeared out of sight.

'The book,' said Ethan pointing to Jack's rucksack which was glowing once again.

The noise coming from further up the path was getting louder and through the fading light they could see a large figure heading in their direction. The approaching figure appeared to be walking on four legs. Had they just been pulled out of the frying pan only to be dropped into the fire? They stayed huddled in their group and as the creature drew nearer it rose onto its two rear legs.

'A polar bear,' whispered Ethan, almost excited now and not fearful as you'd expect.

'Ssshh,' said Jack as the bear approached.

It stood looking over the party. Jack and Abi remained stony faced. Max was curled up in a ball with his paws hiding his head and Ethan, well he just beamed a smile right back at the bear.

Abi launched into a piercing scream, her eyes screwed tightly shut. The bear tilted his head back as she screeched uncontrollably. Astonishingly the bear spoke, 'This is no place for small children,' he said.

Abi's scream came to an abrupt halt; her face was a picture of confusion. The boys' jaws could have hit the floor. They were lost for words, a talking bear. What next?

'I'm Fang,' he said introducing himself. 'Follow me, before those wolves come back.' He lowered himself onto all fours and began walking back up the hill.

The children were still rooted to the spot with shock, but the bear asked a second time as he turned his head. This time they sprang into action and began to follow him up the path.

CHAPTER 14
Fang

FRIDAY, 20TH DECEMBER

Mike had just returned from the station, he'd pretty much spent the last two days at the panicked parent's house. He moved into the lounge and explained to them what they were doing to find the children.

'OK, so we've got a location on the GPS this morning and it's a town in north Scandinavia called Frozen Claw of all places,' he started. 'The nearest police station isn't too far and they sent a couple of officers into town to see what they could find out.'

'Have they found them, have they?' she asked.

'Not exactly,' replied Mike, 'but there have been sightings, or at least we think,' he added.

'It appears that a few of the locals remember the children and their dog. That must be your Max right?' he said.

There was a slight pause

'But?' Dad said, 'I can feel a but coming?'

'But, it appears they left the town first thing this morning with an old retired sheriff,' responded Mike. 'So we're looking for him as we speak.'

Mum turned around to hug Dad, still clearly distressed.

'But at least they've been seen though, isn't that right Mike?' said Dad.

'Yes, yes,' said Mike. 'Any sign is a positive sign, we're making progress here guys, let's stay positive.'

Clearly this was easier said than done, the whole saga was taking a real toll on the parents, but this was at least the first piece of positive news they had received. They would just need to wait for another contact from Abi or Jack.

Back in the North the children and Max had followed Fang up the path and to a series of caves overlooking the wilderness below. The largest of the caves appeared to be Fang's residence. There were many items in there, most of which were old sled parts and some old broken parts of what looked like machinery of sorts. These seemed very odd items to be found out in the wilderness, or at least that's what Abi and Jack thought.

Ethan was still transfixed on Fang. This was like something from his dreams, a real life polar bear, but this one could actually speak. Most people would generally display some form of fear, but to Ethan this was magnificent.

Fang led the three children into the cave, he could see that they were bitterly cold and gathered some scrap pieces of wood together and it appeared he was going to light a fire. Jack reached into his backpack to look for a box of matches he had packed, but as he did Fang ran his claws across a large rock he had placed the timbers by. The sparks flew from his claws and lit up the rock like a firework, enough of the sparks jumped into the makeshift fire and lit the small kindling that were amongst the bigger timbers.

'Very clever!' insisted Abi as she half applauded Fang's skills.

'Why thank you very much,' he replied with an appreciative nod.

'What's wrong with the little guy?' he added looking over at Ethan.

'I think he's in shock,' replied Jack. 'We don't get many polar bears back home, and even less ones that can talk.'

'We can all talk, we just choose when to,' said Fang. 'You guys looked pretty scared down there, particularly the young lady,' he commented looking over at Abi who found herself a little embarrassed as she recollected her panic attack. 'So I thought I'd try and put your mind at ease. So anyway what are you doing all the way out here and how did you get here?' he asked.

'We were looking for you. Tiberius brought us,' said Ethan out of the blue, who'd now come back to the land of the living.

'For me? Why?' said a puzzled Fang.

'The Calendar told us to,' said Jack as he pulled it from his backpack and opened it up. It was once again glowing and he laid it on the ground so they could all see the message that would unfold.

Fang looked intrigued, but appeared to lose interest as no message was appearing. Then, just as it always did, a message slowly revealed itself.

You must ask Fang to take you to the Mystic Forest, to the Gate of Advent, Christmas depends on it.

The page opposite slowly lit up to reveal yet another visual treat and what looked to the children like an enchanted forest. The animation tracked a path through the forest to some kind of magical hedgerow.

Fang sat back slowly.

'Christmas eh…' he said.

'That's a blast from the past, Christmas used to be an important time in my life,' he said, 'but no one's heard of Christmas or anything to do with Christmas for quite some time. I think you guys may be wasting your time.'

'But we've come this far,' Jack said quickly. 'We can't give up now,' he pleaded with the bear.

Ethan and Abi were transfixed by the Calendar, this book was truly extraordinary, the visions it was offering the children were mesmeric and Ethan in particular could not take his eyes off the page.

Fang was clearly confused by the message. Christmas was such a distant memory, but these three children had achieved so much it seemed a shame to not let them continue in their endeavours. The Calendar was persuading him to assist the children in their quest. It had something about it, some magic of Christmases past. It was almost dark and clearly any journey they had to make would have to wait until tomorrow.

'OK,' said Fang. 'We'll head off in the morning. You guys get warm by the fire and have a bite to eat and a rest. I've got something I need to do.' He left for one of the other caves.

The children were relieved that Fang had agreed to help them. Together with Max they sat around the fire keeping it topped up with timber from time to time. Looking around the cave they could establish that Fang must have been some sort of engineer, if indeed bears could be engineers. There were various tools, old and some relatively new, and parts of a variety of old machines and vehicles, but all of them appeared very old as if this was in a past life of his. Clearly though he still kept his hand in as he could be heard working in the adjoining caves.

The three children sat down around the fire and pulled out some food. It took effort to remember to eat with all the excitement of the trip. They could be forgiven for forgetting their meals, but Abi was the sensible one and knew they needed to keep their strength up, particularly in this harsh environment.

Jack placed the Calendar on a shelf before returning to the fire and lying down using his rucksack as a pillow. The other two followed suit and soon all three were sound asleep. The excitement of the day and their exposure to the elements had taken its toll on them.

Fang periodically popped in to see the children and to make sure the fire was burning all night. He was hard at work until the early hours when he too decided to call it a night and get some well earned rest. He made one last check on the children then returned to the other cave and hung the item he had been working on from a hook on the wall. The item had clearly been designed for him to wear and for the children to mount. He was very thoughtful and had considered that the children would be unable to travel on foot and that he would need to somehow carry them the whole way. He lay down to rest; his journey tomorrow would need him at his best.

CHAPTER 15

The Calendar's Gone

SATURDAY, 21ST DECEMBER

Max was barking loudly, it was barely daylight and he was going berserk. Ethan woke first, quickly followed by Jack then Abigail. Just at that moment Fang came in.

'What's all the noise,' he said.

'It's just Max,' replied Ethan. 'I think he got spooked, although he doesn't normally act like this.'

Jack felt uneasy; Max was never like this. He ran to the edge of the cave to look outside but could see nothing. Then he suddenly looked down and saw tracks on the floor.

'Someone was here,' he said.

Fang stood up on his hind legs and went to the cave's entrance looking very menacing indeed. He looked at the tracks and growled. This was his home, who had dared to trespass?

Jack had run back into the cave and was frantically searching, He was going through everything, his bag, Abi's bag, even Fang's 'junk'.

He turned to the others, 'It's gone, it's gone,' he said repeatedly.

His siblings turned to see what he had lost as he continued to search desperately.

'What is it Jack?' asked Abi.

'The Calendar, it's gone!' he yelled.

Fang turned when he heard this revelation and gave instructions to Abi and Ethan, 'You two stay here and keep safe.'

Then he looked at Jack inquisitively, 'You,' he said to Jack firmly, 'get on.' Fang settled down on all fours and faced the entrance to the cave, beckoning Jack to climb on his back. He had decided that Abigail needed to remain behind to take care of Ethan and guard their items along with Max, while he and Jack needed to head off to retrieve the Calendar.

Jack, always up for a challenge, didn't need a second invitation. He rushed over to Fang and grabbed a hold of his fur before throwing his left leg across his back and burying his chest into the rear of Fang's neck, gripping with all his might.

'We'll be back,' said Fang in an almost mock Russian accent, very reminiscent of another famous hero thought Ethan. With that he launched into a thunderous gallop out of the cave and along the path following the tracks of their unknown intruders. It soon became apparent that Max had in fact almost interrupted the thief as they had barely gained an advantage over their pursuers. Fang and Jack had only been on their trail for a few minutes when they caught sight of them.

'There!' called out Jack pointing to a small cluster of dogs pulling a small sled carrying one passenger dressed head to toe in black. With every stride Fang was gaining on the sled. Jack was amazed as to how quickly Fang could move, such a big powerful beast, yet with a real turn of pace.

They were soon within a hundred yards or so of their target and Jack could see the man that much clearer. Somehow the man looked familiar, but Jack couldn't quite place him. The path ahead seemed to be narrowing as it approached a tight bend around the side of the cliff face. The sled and its dogs disappeared round the bend and just fifteen seconds or so later Fang and Jack reached the same bend. Fang slowed as if he was expecting some kind of ambush, he slowed to almost walking pace and began to snarl. Sure enough as they turned the corner they came face to face with their enemies.

The sled had stopped and the dogs had slipped their reins and were standing side by side with their owner behind them. These were no ordinary huskies; these were very dark, almost black and demonic in appearance. They were snarling and salivating as they looked Fang up and down. There were four in total and were bigger than any dogs Jack had ever seen.

Jack was now able to get a clear look at the man who was holding the Calendar. It was Lupus Grimm. Jack remembered seeing him as they pulled out of the store back in town.

'Give that Calendar back,' he yelled, instantly realising that he sounded like a petulant child. Fang gave him a look of almost embarrassment.

'That Calendar does not belong to you Lupus,' said Fang. Clearly he knew who he was dealing with.

'It's not your business Fang, we have no quarrel here,' said Lupus. 'Turn back now and we can forget all of this.'

There was a long pause. Jack wasn't sure what would happen next, after all they hardly knew Fang and clearly he had some sort of history with Lupus Grimm. Luckily he needn't of worried.

'I can't do that, I promised to help these children and I suspect that the mission they are on is of great importance,' he replied. 'I suspect you think so as well.'

'Well, that's just too bad,' countered Lupus.

'Boys,' and with that command the dogs launched themselves towards Fang.

Fang rose onto his hind legs throwing Jack clear. One of the dogs was swiftly swatted aside with a swipe of one of his huge paws, the second was deflected to one side. The third, however, latched onto Fang's rear and snarled furiously as it shook its head vigorously trying to tear the bear's flesh.

Fang spun sharply dislodging the dog before throwing it firmly against the side of the cliff. The other dogs came relentlessly and Fang was engaged in a fierce battle.

Jack stood clear and watched. On the other side of the melee he could see Lupus starting to get away. Jack took up the chase. He was a young, healthy teenager and quickly caught up with Lupus. He tackled him to the ground from behind, catching the older man unawares. Quickly Jack got to his feet, the Calendar had been dropped and he reached for it, but as he did he was grabbed by Lupus.

'You stupid little boy. What do you think you are going to do? Do you think you are going to overpower me?' he said with an arrogant chuckle.

He had Jack by the scruff of the neck and was holding him six inches or so above the ground. Jack struggled frantically, but as he did so Lupus strengthened his grip and began to make his way to the edge of the path. Jack looked around and could see the edge approaching, his expression changed to one of panic.

'You think you can come here and change things around with this stupid Calendar,' he said to Jack. 'I like things as they are. I run things up here and no one's going to change that.'

The edge of the cliff was fast approaching and Jack's time was about to run out. Then out of nowhere they were both thrown sideways. Jack was thrown to relative safety and Lupus was sent tumbling towards the edge of the cliff.

'Max!' yelled Jack. His faithful friend had followed Fang up the path and, although usually very reserved in his actions, he had responded to Jack's desperate plight and thrown himself at the wrestling pair and in doing so changed the fortunes of his owner.

Lupus was left hanging over the cliff edge, with the slope below beckoning, he called out for help.

'Boys, boys,' he called.

Hearing his pleas, the dogs ended their engagement with Fang and ran hurriedly to his rescue. The first dog to reach him took hold of his collar with its teeth and hung on to ensure his master didn't fall. Unfortunately, the other three dogs weren't so clever. They came bounding over and between the three of them got into an almighty mess and ended up colliding with each other and the lead dog, sending them all, including Lupus, tumbling clumsily over the edge and down the steep bank which appeared almost endless.

Jack and Max peered over the edge to catch a glimpse of the group tumbling comically for what seemed an eternity before coming to an abrupt halt at the base of the mountain. They were still in one piece, but were clearly defeated. But would they come again thought Jack?

'They won't be getting far without this,' said Fang as he approached Jack and Max. He was looking at Lupus Grimm's sled, when suddenly with one powerful blow he all but demolished the carriage.

Jack was confused. Yes, he knew Lupus Grimm was an unpleasant character, but why was this Calendar important enough for him to risk his life? And why did Fang suggest their task might be of great importance?

'Why did they do that? Why did they want this Calendar so badly?' asked Jack.

'Lupus has been the big man around here for quite some time now,' replied Fang. 'I guess he doesn't want that to change.'

Jack didn't really understand what Fang meant. Why would this Calendar have an impact on Lupus Grimm, what power lay within this mere book?

Jack looked at Fang inquisitively, waiting for instructions. Fang was carrying the scars of battle; he had been heavily outnumbered and had taken some damage.

'Are you OK?' asked Jack.

'Just a few scratches,' replied a humble Fang. 'Let's head back so we can get this journey started.'

Jack didn't hitch a ride with Fang. He felt the bear had taken enough of a beating. After picking up the Calendar he walked back down to the cave with Max and the heroic bear.

'Jack, Fang, Max!' called out Abi and Ethan as the trio approached the cave.

Fang was visibly injured and Abi rushed to his side to offer help.

'Are you OK? Let me take a look at you,' she said as she started to inspect his injuries. Fang looked confused, he clearly wasn't used to this attention and Abi was an expert when it came to mothering people.

'I'll be fine. I just need to rest for a little… but thank you for caring,' he added, smiling for the first time since they had met. With that he settled down inside the cave for a well-earned rest. Ethan was curious as to what had taken place and would not let Jack rest until he was given a full account of the event that had just passed. He listened intently as Jack described the battle word for word, but the one part of the story Ethan really found to his liking was the tale of Max's intervention.

'I knew you had it in you Max,' said Ethan as he made a real fuss of his trusty friend who had really come to their rescue this day. The three children sat down inside the cave, the overnight fire still had a few bright embers and they were glad of its warmth. Fang was soon in a deep sleep, his snoring resonating around the cave walls.

'Do you think he'll be OK?' asked Ethan.

'I'm sure he will, it would take a lot to knock him back, you should have seen him,' said Jack. Fang had gone above and beyond the call of duty for their cause already, and he was still intent on completing his leg of the journey.

'Have you remembered to message home Abs?' asked Ethan.

With all the chaos of the night before and the frightening episode with the wolves Abi had forgotten to send her daily message to her Mum and Dad. She pulled her mobile out of her pack, but unsurprisingly there was no signal.

'No reception here,' she said clearly frustrated. 'I'll try again a little later when we've started to move.'

Back home Mike was doing his best to reassure Mum and Dad.

'We've got people searching near Frozen Claw,' he explained to the exasperated parents.

'We know, Mike, and we're grateful, but with every hour that passes we are losing hope,' replied Dad. That evening having no message had taken a real toll on them, they were sleeping less and less each night and the chances of the children being found unharmed appeared to be falling. Had they known about the wolves, Lupus Grimm and the fact the children were sleeping in a cave with a wild polar bear, they would have gone out of their minds.

Mike, however, was now starting to fear the worst. His counterparts up near Frozen Claw had made him aware of the harsh environment. Three children stuck in the wilderness in those conditions would surely not fare well, even experienced explorers found these conditions challenging.

'Listen guys,' he said, 'I'm going to head back to the station and see what's happening there.' He said goodbye and headed back to the town centre. Mum and Dad had little option but to wait for news, they felt so helpless, so powerless, the children were their whole lives and right now those lives were in the balance.

CHAPTER 16
All Aboard the Bear

SATURDAY, 21ST DECEMBER

After a couple of hours rest Fang woke. He was clearly a heavy sleeper but once awake that was that, he was fresh and ready to go.

'Right, it's time we made a move. Just give me a minute,' he added as he left for one of the adjoining caves.

Jack looked at Abi and Ethan inquisitively.

'He looks OK?' he said. Amazingly Fang appeared to be carrying no signs of injury other than the superficial wounds.

'Then I guess you were right,' replied Abi.

Fang returned to the children carrying what looked like a harness of sorts, this was clearly what he had been busy working on into the early hours of the morning. He lowered the harness onto his back and asked the children to help tie up the straps.

The harness had three seating positions, one behind the other and a sort of side pouch to the left. Once the harness was fastened tightly he instructed the children to climb aboard. The seats had small handles for the children to grip onto to ensure a safe ride. Ethan was instructed to sit at the front which delighted him, he felt he was in charge of this ride. Clearly none of the children were in control, Fang was the master of this journey.

Max looked suitably confused as the children sat atop the powerful bear. Fang turned to the dog. 'This one's for you,' he said tilting his head in the direction of the pouch on his left hand side. Max looked up at Jack looking for some sort of confirmation.

'Come on boy,' Jack said and with that Max took his position in the pouch made of strong netting. As they took their fist steps Abi caught their reflection in a sheet of ice at the edge of the cave. What a strange sight they were, three children and a dog being chauffeured by a talking polar bear, you couldn't make this up she thought!

Fang was an incredibly steady creature; he was as solid as a rock and showed no signs of tiredness as he carried the group further up the path before taking a downhill route towards the rear of the mountain.

The route down was quite a bit steeper than the path they had followed up the side of the mountain, but Fang was very sure footed and soon carried his passengers to level ground. Once the terrain flattened out he took up more of a trot than previously and they started to make good ground on their journey to the Mystic Forest.

'How far is it?' asked Ethan as he tried to catch his breath. The front seat as it turned out wasn't quite so advantageous, it was like sticking your head out of a window in a moving car, but only this car was in freezing conditions.

'Just a few hours,' replied Fang. 'But the path isn't quite so straightforward further on.'

Indeed the path was about to change quite dramatically as they approached the edge of what appeared to be a lake, or perhaps even a channel. The water was mainly ice but there were a few gaps that had some floating blocks of ice patrolling them. Fang stopped at the water's edge, surveying the ice and the various gaps they would need to negotiate. Clearly he was looking for the easiest route, if indeed there was a route at all.

He settled on a path and started to make his way slowly along the ice. If he had been alone, then these waters would have held no fear for him, a stumble here and there and a fall through the ice into the water would not usually be a problem with his thick fur. This time, however, he could not afford such a slip, these children could not fall into the water as the cold would surely put them in grave danger. So he moved slowly, almost testing the ice with each step.

'I can't look, I can't look,' said Abi burying her head in Fang's back. Fang was in no mood for a comedy repost and remained focused on his task. They made their way along a small path in one of the breaks in the ice, almost like an ice bridge. Suddenly there was a cracking sound, Fang stopped in his tracks, but it was too late. The ice they were standing on broke away from the rest and they began to drift. The piece of ice was tilting from one side to the other and Fang was constantly adjusting his stance to keep aboard the runaway block.

The children were remarkably calm, although Abi had no idea what was going on as she hadn't looked up for quite some time. Ethan seemed to be enjoying himself, believing it was like a fairground ride, clearly unaware of the danger they were in. Fang struggled with his balance, rocking one way then the other, his rear left foot slipped and entered the freezing water. He quickly adjusted himself and established his position once again. Fortunately the small iceberg they were drifting on was heading back to the large body of ice from which it had broken free. It came to rest alongside the main glacier and Fang carefully made his way back onto more solid ground.

The next hour or so was a continuation of the same theme, solid ground, to drifting ice, to solid ground. Fang became more confident in his ferrying skills as time progressed and with this confidence his pace slowly picked up. The body of water was soon crossed and the group were trotting across the tundra for a mile or so when in the distance a forest beckoned.

'Is that it, is that it?' asked Jack, at which point Abi lifted her head.

'That's Brennin Forest,' replied Fang. 'Mystic's on the other side.'

They approached the forest and Fang's pace slowed, he was happy to travel through the forest at a more leisurely pace. Brennin Forest was magnificent, tall pine trees had scattered cones all over the forest floor. The strong green colour of the pine trees was even more apparent against the background of the white landscape.

The children were now all sitting up tall, taking in all of the forest that surrounded them, it reminded them a little of home and the woods they played in. Fang crunched and snapped his way over twigs and branches, clearly unfazed by the splinters and sharp edges. They were about half or mile or so into the forest when Abi started to have the uneasy feeling that they were being watched. She was looking around frantically to try and ease her worries.

'What's up Abs?' asked Jack to his irritated sister.

'Um… nothing,' she said. 'Just looking round,' trying not to pass on her fears. Surely Lupus Grimm was not on their trail again. How did he cross the lake? He couldn't have, she thought. She hoped beyond hope that he hadn't returned. The others had no such fears, they were contentment personified as they wandered gently through the woods.

It wasn't long before they could see beyond the trees on the far side of Brennin Forest. They couldn't quite make out what was ahead, the only thing they could see through the branches was the white of yet more snow, but that was hardly unexpected.

They broke through the far edge of the forest and into a small clearing, on the other side of the clearing was another forest.

'There's Mystic Forest,' said Fang. The children sat upright trying to take in the view.

'But we have a problem,' explained Fang. The children looked down in front of where they stood; their hearts dropped at what they saw. There was a huge chasm between them and the Mystic Forest. They looked left and they looked right, the chasm seemed to stretch on beyond where the eye could see. What now? Was this a dead end?

'Is there a bridge? A way round?' Jack asked Fang.

'Not that I know of,' he replied. 'You sure you read that book right?'

Jack turned round and reached for his pack, pulling out the Calendar. He opened up the page where they had read the message. Once again the message read the same:

You must ask Fang to take you to the Mystic Forest, to the Gate of Advent, Christmas depends on it.

'We need to get to the Gate of Advent,' said Jack.

Fang looked confused. 'There's the forest, that much I do know, but that gate you talk of, I don't recall ever hearing its name before,' he said.

This didn't make sense, if Fang didn't know where the gate was and the children didn't know, then how were they supposed to find it?

The children climbed down from Fang's back. All three stretched their legs like people stepping out of a car after a long journey. Ethan helped Max from his 'pouch', the poor dog was almost frozen stiff, his coat was not equipped for these conditions and he decided perhaps they needed to consider his well being a little more. Max shook himself vigorously and a few small lumps of ice that had formed in his coat were sent flying to the sides as he shook the cold from his limbs.

Abi kept her eyes firmly on the forest behind, still not convinced that Lupus Grimm was no longer on their trail. She'd had this nagging feeling whilst travelling though Brennin Forest that they were being watched.

Fang sat down, clearly racking his brain trying to recall ever hearing of a 'gate' in the Mystic Forest. Ethan was peering into the deep chasm; there was no apparent way of crossing to the other side. The edge was virtually sheer and there was no way of lowering themselves down, the drop was sixty or seventy feet at least.

'Come and look at this drop Jack,' said Ethan excitedly as he tossed a snowball into the chasm. Just as Jack was approaching Ethan heard a cracking sound come from the forest behind them. They all turned quickly and Fang rose to his feet.

'What was that?' asked Abi. 'I knew it, I knew it,' she added.

Fang looked at her confused.

'What do you mean?' asked Jack.

'I felt someone was watching us, Lupus Grimm must have followed us,' she replied.

With that Fang rose tall and began to snarl. He thought Lupus had been dealt with, but he was more than ready for round two. Another crack as something moved closer to them, then another, not exactly moving at much pace but clearly closing in on them. The children stepped behind Fang with just their heads peering out to the sides. Max, however, stood alongside Fang, with a newfound confidence.

They could now see a figure approaching through the trees but it was hard to make out who or what it was. The figure started to become clearer and clearer. It was certainly not human, but also didn't appear particularly threatening.

The groups' mood seemed to change, they were now less worried and more curious. What was this creature in Brennin Forest? It soon became crystal clear as the creature's antlers pushed through the trees as it stepped out into the clearing. An old reindeer stood motionless looking the group over. It was hard to tell who was more confused, the silence was suddenly broken by Fang's laughter.

'Rudy old friend,' he said walking over to greet the reindeer. Max also walked over, leaving the children standing together, still utterly confused.

Fang turned to them.

'Don't worry, this is Rudolph, an old, old friend. We haven't seen each other for years,' he said. Clearly the two were acquaintances although the reindeer didn't have the power of speech like his bear friend, just the odd grunt here and groan there, but he seemed to understand what Fang was saying to him.

The children had no idea what their next step should be. They were at the mercy of Fang as he was the expert and someone they had to rely on. Fang though was almost out of ideas when he suddenly had a thought.

'Rudolph, you're well acquainted with these parts,' he said. 'Have you heard of the… what's the gate called?' he added looking at Jack and Abi.

'The umm… Gate of Advent,' replied Abi hesitantly.

Rudolph nodded. Then he pushed his nose forward in the direction of the Mystic Forest.

'We kind of knew it was over there Rudy,' responded Fang. 'But do you know exactly where?'

Again Rudolph nodded. The children now had someone who knew exactly where they were heading, this was progress indeed, but still there was no suggestion of how they could cross to the forest. Rudolph clearly understood that the children were in need of help and he lowered himself by kneeling on his two front legs. He beckoned Jack towards him. Jack stepped forward. He then turned his head to the rear clearly instructing Jack to mount him, Jack obliged.

'Does he know a way round?' Jack asked Fang.

'In a way,' replied Fang with a strange look in his eyes.

Suddenly Rudolph turned back towards Brennin Forest and, with Jack on his back, trotted back into the trees and out of sight.

'What the…?' said Abi. Suddenly she and Ethan both panicked and Max began to bark. Had their brother just been snatched from them, what was going on? Fang seemed quite relaxed about the whole situation which confused Abi and Ethan greatly, even Max had a confused look on his face as he turned to Fang and stopped barking.

Suddenly Rudolph returned but at a real pace, he was running flat out across the clearing headed for the chasm. Jack was wrapped around the reindeer holding tight, his eyes tightly shut. Just as the reindeer approached the edge of the drop Jack suddenly had a feeling of weightlessness. He opened his eyes only to see that Rudolph had leapt from the edge of the chasm and was climbing steadily through the air.

Back on solid ground Abi and Ethan's faces were a picture; jaws agape, clearly stunned by what they had just witnessed.

'Still got it!' shouted Fang to his friend as he flew across the chasm, before coming down on the other side and lowering himself to allow Jack to dismount. Rudolph returned to transport the other children and Max one by one to the other side of the canyon. However, just before Ethan would climb on board the reindeer he ran across to Fang, disappearing in his midriff as he gave him a heartfelt hug. He had realised that Rudolph would not be helping Fang cross to the Mystic Forest and this would be the end of his part in their journey.

'Thanks for everything,' said Ethan, his voice muffled by a face full of fur.

'You're welcome,' replied Fang. 'I hope everything works out OK for you.'

With that Ethan returned to the reindeer and climbed on his back before being delivered safely to his siblings. The three of them shouted goodbye to Fang and waved vigorously. Jack was a little upset that he hadn't been given a proper chance to say goodbye, he felt that he and Fang had formed some special bond during their tussle with Lupus and his hounds, but had a feeling he may yet see the bear again.

Fang slowly turned and trudged off back into Brennin Forest. The children and Max were now standing on the edge of the Mystic Forest, with a new guide to lead the way.

CHAPTER 17
Mystic Forest

SATURDAY, 21ST DECEMBER

Standing looking up at the tall trees on the edge of the forest the group understood why this forest had been given its name. The trees seemed to have a strange glow about them and an almost magical presence.

Rudolph slowly led the way, steadily entering into the forest and crossing its pine needle-covered floor. The children wondered at what they saw in the forest; the trees were dressed with pieces of moss and vines that were silverfish in colour and decorated the trees beautifully. The pine needle floor almost felt like it had been carpeted with the most luxurious shag pile. The visual treat was complemented by the beautiful scent of the forest, the powerful smell of spruce trees combined with what seemed like sweet apples, not that there were any visible signs of that sort of vegetation. This place was truly out of this world and absolutely enchanting.

In such beautiful surroundings the children lost all sense of time. It was now early evening and the sun had set some time ago, yet the forest was well lit with the silver foliage and the moon up above providing a most magical light.

The children looked at each other inquisitively.

'How far is it?' asked Ethan, not really expecting an answer; the question was more out of habit than anything.

'What do you think?' replied Jack sarcastically, with a small chuckle in his voice. 'We'll just follow Rudolph until we get there I guess.'

They were in no rush, even children of their tender ages were able to appreciate how magnificent this place was, they would surely never see its like again. From time to time they would come across other reindeer feeding in the forest, they simply looked up, gave the children the once over and carried on grazing.

'A squirrel!' said Ethan excitedly as he watched a brightly coloured red squirrel climb quickly up one of the pine trees. Surely this part of the world was too cold for squirrels thought Abi, but then nothing was what it seemed in these parts. A talking bear, a flying reindeer, surely a travelling squirrel wasn't beyond the realms of possibility.

One thing that did have the children guessing, was the occasional snowman they came across from time to time, perfectly built, well designed with twigs for arms, what looked like black pebbles for eyes and carrots for noses. Who had built these and when? Abi rationalised that they must have been built years ago by people travelling through the forest and clearly would never have had cause to melt. Jack wasn't convinced, although he wasn't actually that interested. Ethan on the other hand was dubious, and swore that on more than one occasion the eyes of some of these snowmen had moved and followed their path.

In spite of the presence of these snowmen the forest itself was strangely warm; not warm so much, but not as cold as the rest of the landscape, it was almost as if it had its own climate. Yes, there was snow on part of the ground but the forest itself was certainly somewhere where the children felt as comfortable as they had for a while.

Up ahead, the path Rudolph was following seemed to end and there was a dense patch of trees with no apparent way through. It looked like a bush tree with silvery vines hanging from it in some strange pattern, criss-cross in parts and in columns in others.

Rudolph's pace started to slow, not that it had ever been quick, but certainly he was slowing down. He stopped just a few yards in front of the dense trees. He looked at the children and tilted his head at the dead end. Was this the way forward or was he simply pointing out that this was a dead end and he had done all he could? With the tilt of his head Rudolph turned around nonchalantly and started heading back the way they had just come.

The children started to panic, were they being abandoned? What would they do now? This was the first time they had been alone since they arrived in Frozen Claw. At least that town had been inhabited, albeit with some unsavoury characters, this forest though, apart from some wildlife, was deserted.

Once again, Jack put his backpack on the floor and sure enough the Calendar was forthcoming and started to glow brightly through the waterproof material.

'Did you ever doubt it?' asked Abi with a sense of relief.

Jack pulled out the Calendar as Ethan and Abi gathered round. They all sat on a fallen tree with a covering of soft moss which actually made for a very comfortable seat.

Jack opened the book and an amazing illustrated picture of Mystic Forest appeared, showing the forest in all its glory, then the message:

Call out the name of Father Christmas and let the Gate of Advent lead you to his home.

The adjoining page showed a view from above the trees or hedgerow ahead, it showed them lighting up peculiarly and opening from the centre revealing a wintery path ahead.

Abi looked at the boys. 'Do we just shout it out?' she asked.

'I'm not s...' Jack hadn't had time to finish his sentence before Ethan was screaming 'Father Christmas' at the top of his voice. Over and over he called out, but nothing changed.

'Maybe try Santa or something else,' proposed Abi. The three of them called out a variety of options, Santa, Santa Claus, Father Christmas, they even started using some foreign versions of his name Ethan had stored on his tablet before they left.

Sion Corn, Weihnachtsmann, Père Fouettard, the Welsh, German and French equivalents were just some of the names they called. Abi, as particular as ever, wasn't happy with their pronunciation on several of the names, but the boys just kept churning out the different names as Abi more deliberately called out her versions.

They continued to call these out for almost twenty minutes when they stopped to revise their strategy.

'Why can't things be more straightforward?' said Jack. He enjoyed a world where things were much more black and white, not cryptic like this journey they were undertaking. Abi was holding her phone aloft in various positions trying to get some sort of signal. She was anxious that she had been unable to contact home now for quite some time and could only imagine the anguish her parents were feeling.

'Still nothing?' inquired Jack.

'Useless,' she replied. 'Although look where we are,' she added, rolling her eyes. She had managed to establish the time, it was now almost seven o'clock and she was getting worried about them being out overnight. Yes, the forest was a lot more habitable than the other parts of their journey to date, but it surely wasn't somewhere they needed to be spending the night alone.

Ethan was scrolling through various pages in his documents searching for clues, whilst munching on almost the last of his food supplies. The three of them had hardly sat down to eat at all during their adventure, but had eaten sporadically and, with the exception of Abi, were almost out of rations.

Ethan looked up, 'Do you know what I'd kill for now?'

'Go on then…. what?' replied Abi.

'One of those hot chocolates,' he replied.

There was a slight delay before the other two said simultaneously as if they had planned to, 'Old Kris' chocolate' .

No sooner had they uttered those words than Max became agitated, he had turned to face the trees and started barking. The children turned around, there was movement in the tightly bunched trees before them. The silvery vines started to shift, settling in positions one at a time, like an elaborate sort of combination lock.

It was only thirty seconds or so, although it seemed much longer, until the vine, or at least what looked like vines, settled into place. What had looked like a cluster of trees and other foliage now resembled an organic gate of sorts with the silver vines resembling metal railings and posts, almost regal in appearance.

They stood staring at the structure in awe, they had no idea what words or name had led to this transformation, they could only assume the effort Ethan had made with his various versions of Santa Claus had paid off.

'Well done Eth,' said Jack, praising his little brother even if he wasn't absolutely certain who had successfully revealed the gate. The gate, however, was still closed and, unlike the usual type of grand gate this one resembled, there was no way to see through the railings.

'What should we do?' Jack asked Abi.

'Not sure,' she replied. 'Just give it a minute or so.'

Just as the revealing of the gate had taken time and the messages in the Calendar were slow in appearing, Abi thought they should wait to see if the gate opened of its own accord. A minute passed, then five, then ten. Jack was impatient.

'I think I should try and open it,' he said.

Abi wasn't sure, there was no sign of a handle, no sign of anything that resembled a handle. She couldn't find any reason now for Jack not to try.

'OK, give it a go,' she said.

Jack stepped forwards to the middle of the gate. He reached just left of centre and into a dense section of small branches covered in gentle green pine needles. His hand disappeared right up to the elbow on his left arm. He could feel some kind of knob and he turned it. The gate made a sound and then it started to shift slowly. Jack took a step or two back and watched with the rest of the group as both gate and leaves slowly swung back.

Were they perhaps approaching the end of their journey, or was this just another step along their curious route?

CHAPTER 18
Contact

SATURDAY, 21ST DECEMBER

'It was now just after eight o'clock at night and the children stood motionless staring through the open gate. Ahead was a long, straight road, slightly uphill, almost as far as the eye could see. The road was flanked either side by walls reminiscent of country lane dry stone walls but a little higher than normal, perhaps eight or nine feet. The walls were pretty rustic and had certainly been built by hand and not machine.

The road itself was a blanket of white snow with no footprints or blemishes, so clearly had not been followed in recent times. Conscious that time was against them, Abi asked the boys to gather their things and pick up their bags. Ethan just had time to remove a small treat from his pack for Max, who was grateful for the energy out in these cold conditions.

The four of them headed along the path at a fairly brisk pace. The path was a steady climb, although not too steep as to tire the children excessively. They had been walking for about twenty minutes when out of the corner of his eye Jack noticed that they had company. He stopped in his tracks, quickly followed by Ethan and Abi. They turned to their right and looked up, on top of the wall, dressed in what looked like a green onesie with red trimming and a pointy red hat stood a small man, or was it a boy? He was no more than four foot or so it seemed. It wasn't easy to tell exactly from down on the path but indeed he was no ordinary man.

He looked down at them blankly. The children appeared comfortable in his presence and they showed no fear.

'Hello,' said Ethan.

'Ssshh,' said Abi.

The man did not reply, he just stood there expressionless. The children waited for a couple of minutes before looking at each other and continuing on their route. The small man followed them along the top of the wall. They walked a further thirty yards or so and stopped, all of them looking quickly up to the wall where the small man had also stopped. They repeated this a couple times and each time was the same, the effect was quite comical as the small man mirrored their actions. Just at that moment Abi's phoned buzzed in her backpack.

'I've got a signal,' she said, accidentally dropping her pack to the floor behind her as she wriggled to take it off quickly. She rummaged furiously before finding her phone and pulling it out. With the way the signal had been and her inability, or any of the children's inability, to let their parents know they were safe, Abi thought they deserved something a bit more substantial. She wanted to phone.

She looked at the boys before announcing her intentions.

'I want to call home,' she said.

The boys looked at each other.

'Do you think we should?' replied Jack. 'We can't tell them where we are or what we're doing remember.'

'I know, I know,' Abi said. 'But we could just let them hear our voices.'

The boys agreed, although strangely Ethan pointed out the expense of such a phone call.

'I can't believe you're the one thinking practically,' Jack said as he laughed at Ethan's sombre input. Abi's phone had some foreign network providers name across her screen and she wasn't sure if she had to dial some sort of international code. She plumped for simply using her contact list and calling her 'home' contact.

The two boys gathered round pushing their ears towards the handset. It was a few seconds before they started to hear a ringtone, not the normal ringtone, but long drawn out rings with small gaps between them.

At home Mum was fast asleep on the sofa downstairs, Dad was in the kitchen talking to Mike. The computer technician heard the phone buzzing and placed his hand on Gwen's shoulder to give her a gentle nudge. She woke suddenly to find he was holding the phone up to her face. Abi's name was lit up across it. She sat up quickly, perhaps a little too quickly as she shook her head in an attempt to get her bearings.

'Josh!' she shouted though to the kitchen. 'Josh!' she repeated. He dashed through to the lounge where he could see her with the phone to her ear.

'Abi? Abi darling are you there?' she said in desperation.

'Hi Mum,' said a voice. With that Mum burst into tears and handed the phone over to her husband as she sobbed uncontrollably.

'Abi?' said Dad.

'Hi Dad,' replied Abi. 'Where did Mum go?'

'Where are you, where are the boys?' asked Dad ignoring Abi's question.

'They're here,' she replied.

'Hi Dad,' called out the boys as they were listening in on the conversation.

'Oh, thank God!' said Dad as he sank down onto the sofa. Covering the phone with his hand he whispered to his wife and the others, 'They're all OK.'

He returned to the phone call, 'Where are you Abi?' he asked. 'You've had us all so worried. I'll come and get you.'

'I'm not exactly sure where we are Dad, but we still have something we need to do. I just hated thinking of you being so worried,' she replied.

'Now listen here,' Dad's tone changed slightly. 'You have to tell me where you all are and I'll come to get you. This is non-negotiable,' he insisted.

Abi looked at the boys, they weren't ready to go home yet, but weren't too keen on disobeying their father either. Perhaps by now they had realised why they shouldn't have phoned home, a message would have been far easier.

'I'm sorry Dad, we still have something we need to do, but just to let you know that you don't need to worry, we're all OK,' said Abi as she hung up. With that she tossed the phone to Jack, as if it was a hot potato. Of all the children Abi was least likely to disobey her parents, so this was out of character for her. Jack held down the power button on the phone to switch it off.

'Abi… Abi?' called out Dad back at home. He pulled the phone away from his face to look at the screen; it was now obvious that the call had ended.

Mum looked up at her husband inquisitively.

'They've gone,' he said.

Mike was very positive about the call, clearly the children were in one piece and they hadn't sounded upset or stressed in anyway. If anything the adults were shocked as to how composed Abi had sounded. These were young children stuck out in a great wilderness, or at least that's what they imagined.

Back in Mystic Forest, Abi wasn't at all comfortable with what she had just done.

'That was horrible,' said Abi. 'I hated talking to Dad like that.'

'Well, at least perhaps they'll worry a bit less now,' Jack suggested.

'I suppose so,' she replied.

The three children had almost forgotten about the company they now had. Max, however, had not taken his eyes off their little 'shadow'. The children all looked up at their follower, clearly untroubled by his presence. Abi put her pack back on and the group set off again along the long, snow-covered path.

It was now just after nine o'clock. Abi was conscious that they needed to complete this leg of their journey as soon as possible, they certainly didn't want to be stuck outside overnight. They were now some distance clear of the forest and its relative warmth. After about another ten or fifteen minutes of walking, Ethan pulled on Jack's sleeve.

'What is it Eth?' asked Jack. Ethan looked up to the wall where there were now two small people following the group. Another small man or boy had joined their original follower and both were walking carefully across the top of the rustic wall, carefully stepping from stone to stone. Abi had also noticed the extra company they had attracted but the unthreatening nature of these small characters meant they were all relatively comfortable just carrying on with their travels.

The number of followers did not end with two, as the children progressed along the path the number of small men on the wall gradually increased. In fact small women started to appear as well, all dressed from head to toe in green and red. Before long their numbers had surpassed twenty and the children were clearly attracting attention.

Abi and Jack were deep in conversation as they walked.

'Who do you think they are?' she asked Jack about their wall-topping guests.

'No idea,' he replied, 'but at least it suggests there's got to be some kind of town or something nearby.'

That idea was a real comfort to the group as a whole. Indeed it wasn't long before they could start to see a glow from over the horizon, well at least the small horizon at the top of the path. They pushed onwards until they neared the top. The numbers of followers had grown substantially over the last few minutes and they now were in excess of one hundred.

The children reached the highest point of the path and ahead of them could now see their destination, and what a destination it was.

CHAPTER 19
The Village

A wonderfully festive, beautifully decorated village lay before the children. They had stopped at the high point of the path to take in what was ahead of them. They could see that the wall that ran alongside the path now opened up and spread out around the perimeter of the settlement. The village itself was made up of small, cosy cottages with the occasional larger building dotted amongst them. Standing tall in what appeared to be the centre of the village was a large clock, not exactly Big Ben, but in this scaled down village, it clearly stood out.

The children were now being watched by what seemed like hundreds of these small people, all dressed similarly, like some small army. Many stood up on the walls either side of them, but now there was a crowd standing at the end of the path at the entrance to the village.

The children didn't really know what to think, or what to do. Abi took both boys by the hand and started to walk slowly down the slope towards the village. They were slightly nervous but walked on putting any negative thoughts to the back of their minds. This place didn't feel like Frozen Claw, which was a cold and unwelcoming place, this small town was almost the opposite, but as yet they had not actually made any form of contact with the inhabitants.

They were only about twenty yards or so from the main entrance and the crowd of men and women when one of the small people stepped forward. It was a man, slightly taller than the rest, but still very small in stature. The children stopped unsure of what was coming.

'Welcome,' he said.

That word was music to their ears, they had not been made particularly welcome on their journey so far, except for Tiberius' and Fang's hospitality that is.

'Hello,' replied Jack.

There was a bit of an awkward silence for thirty seconds or so, almost as if neither party knew who should speak next. One of the other small people gave their 'leader' a nudge, he then continued with an introduction.

'I'm Bernard,' he said, 'Head Elf.'

'Elf?' said Ethan curiously, reaching for his tablet.

'Hello,' said Abi. 'My name is Abi and these are my brothers Ethan and Jack.' Max whined slightly, 'Oh and this is our dog Max.'

Ethan was sure he had heard the term Elf before and was searching through the Christmas facts they had researched when looking for clues.

'Welcome to Santa's village,' said Bernard, 'What can we do for you?'

Santa's Village! The children looked at each other excitedly. Surely this was their intended destination. Should they reveal all or should they keep their cards close to their chest? The children weren't really sure what they were supposed to do, Abi decided they should not rush into anything.

'We're on a journey,' responded Abi, 'but we're in need of somewhere to stay for the night in all honesty.'

Bernard whispered to the female Elf to his left.

'Of course, of course,' he replied, 'you'll stay with me and my wife, Susan.'

A few of the elves approached the children and started to pull at their backpacks; this didn't go down too well with Jack who was resisting quite firmly.

Bernard could see that the children were worried.

'Let us take your bags,' he said. 'It's late in the evening, you must be hungry.'

Ethan and Abi were happy to let their bags be carried, Ethan was too engrossed in his tablet and Abi was glad of the help. Jack, however, insisted he hung on to his, the Calendar was in there and he didn't want it leaving his side.

Bernard led the children to the centre of the village where there was a square in which the clock stood and just beyond it to what must have been his home. The village itself was absolutely spotless, the floor was covered in a heavy blanket of snow and all the houses were lit up beautifully. The colours of the lights and the feel of the whole village reminded Abi very much of old Kris' house back in Willow Cove. Apart from a few small elf children who had stayed to watch, the rest of the elves had either gone back into their cottages or had crossed the square and entered a large building that looked like some sort of warehouse or factory.

'Are you sure you have room for us?' asked Abi as Bernard led them to his door.

'Plenty,' he replied. 'Well, it might be a bit of a squeeze but we'll manage I'm sure.'

Jack went first followed by Ethan and then Abi. Bernard and Sue's house was remarkable. Very modest in size, but extremely welcoming and homely. There was a fire burning in the fireplace and stockings hanging from the mantelpiece. There were candles burning throughout the room and a sweet smell coming from what must have been the kitchen.

Ethan's head lifted from his tablet, 'What's that smell?' he asked, nosy as ever.

'That's my mulled wine,' replied Sue. 'But I think you guys may be a little young for that.'

'Would you like some food?' asked Bernard. 'Or perhaps some hot chocolate?'

The three of them nodded and Bernard disappeared next door to make some drinks.

'While he's making that, let me show you to your room,' Sue suggested.

The children followed her up the small staircase, Jack and Abi had to duck a little to climb the stairs, Ethan, however, had no such issues, he was perfectly built for this place. Their room was remarkably spacious; there was a bunk bed on one wall and a single bed underneath the window. Abi looked out of the window that overlooked the square. The view was fantastic. She could see some elven children having a snowball fight and others pulling each other around on small sleds. The village had such a happy feel to it and was so fantastically picturesque.

'I'll leave you to get settled in,' said Sue. 'Bernie will call you when your drinks are ready.' With that she pulled the door closed behind her and headed back downstairs.

Ethan had finally found the reference to elves on his tablet and was keen to share his information.

'Jack, Abs,' he said, attempting to get their attention.

They both turned round to listen.

'These elves are the people that used to live with Santa Claus,' he started.

'They used to help him make all his presents and help him with the whole Christmas thing.'

'Well, this is Santa's village, this must be where Santa lives,' responded Abi. 'He's got to be here somewhere.'

Jack placed his pack on the bed and pulled out the Calendar, surely it would have information for them. There was, however, no glow, not even the faintest hint of a glow.

'Nothing!' said Jack, clearly frustrated at their lack of direction.

'Well, perhaps we should just settle down for tonight, have a good rest and start again tomorrow,' suggested Abi.

'I guess so,' replied Jack. There was a knock at the door and Sue started to open it, Jack threw his pack over the Calendar in an attempt to cover it.

'Here are your packs,' she said handing Ethan and Abi their rucksacks.

'I see you've got yours,' she said to Jack. Sue looked at his backpack and could see the corner of the Calendar sticking out underneath.

'Come down when you're ready, your drinks are almost done,' she said as she closed the door behind her.

'Did she see it?' asked Jack.

'I don't think so,' replied Abi.

'Maybe?' added Ethan who was not being particularly helpful as usual.

They heard the front door slam shut downstairs. Abi ran to the window. She could see Sue walking hurriedly across the square, had they been rumbled? Had they come all this way only to be stopped in their tracks?

'What is it Abs?' asked Jack.

Abi was keen to play down her suspicions and wanted her brothers to have a peaceful night's sleep.

'Nothing,' she said. 'Just some kids playing.'

The three of them went downstairs where Bernard was sitting in his armchair.

'Take a seat you three, your drinks are on the table,' he said ushering the children to the sofa.

'There's one in there for you boy,' he said to Max, who quickly disappeared into the kitchen and could be heard lapping up some drink or other.

The children sat down and simultaneously picked up their drinks and took a sip. Heaven, that's the only word that could be used to describe the hot chocolate they were given. The three of them sat back, eyes shut, as if they were in some hedonistic state. They had only once before tasted something this amazing, they looked at each other curiously, this drink was identical to the one Old Kris had given them last weekend.

'This chocolate is amazing,' said Abi, 'Where do you get it?'

'It's a secret recipe from here in Santa's Village,' said Bernard. 'Can't give away our secrets,' he added chuckling to himself.

The children again looked at each other. What a strange coincidence they thought, they were sure that the drinks were the same, but perhaps they were just two very good hot chocolates from two very different places.

'Where has Sue gone?' asked Abi, trying to establish whether they had been rumbled or not.

'She's on a night shift in the factory,' replied Bernard.

'Factory?' asked Jack

'Yes, we work hard this month every year, making toys,' Bernard revealed.

'Toys?' Ethan's ears pricked up. 'For who?'

'Well, that's a good question,' said Bernard. 'In recent times, for no one, it's just what we do.'

This didn't really make much sense to the children, why would they make toys if they weren't being used? Bernard went on to explain that each year they spent time making toys, but for some years now they had not been delivered. They were kept in storage in several large warehouses on the far side of town.

'Could you show us?' asked Jack.

'It's much too late now,' replied Bernard. 'Perhaps I could show you round tomorrow?' he suggested.

'Yes, yes,' said Ethan excitedly.

'Only if you have time,' said Abi, giving Ethan a bit of a nudge in the ribs, far more polite in her response.

Bernard offered the children some food, which they politely accepted. After half an hour or so, and after Ethan had demolished three mince pies for his desert, they headed upstairs for a well-earned rest. Later that night, after the children had gone to sleep Sue returned.

'Are they asleep?' she asked Bernard.

'Yes, they went up some time ago,' he replied. 'What did she say?'

'She thought I must be mistaken, but she promised to come over tomorrow afternoon. She's touring the warehouse in the morning, so she'll come over after that,' replied Sue.

Bernard went on to explain how he'd promised to show the children round the factory in the morning, and that he would ensure they were still around in the afternoon for their mystery woman to visit.

CHAPTER 20
Toys, Toys, Toys

SUNDAY, 22ND DECEMBER

Ethan woke first the next morning, he could hear some commotion and some laughter coming from outside. He tumbled out of the bottom half of the bunk bed and staggered across to Abi's bed. He knelt down at the foot of her bed and looked out of the window.

What he saw were dozens of people engaged in tomfoolery, adults and children alike. They were having snowball fights, building snowmen, making snow angels and so much more. Ethan couldn't keep his eyes off the action. Watching though wasn't enough, so he quickly put his waterproofs back on. They had dried well overnight on the radiator and he quickly disappeared downstairs and out through the front door. He was met by a huge snowball, he tried to duck but was too slow, it caught him flush on the cheek.

'Got you!' shouted a small elven child as she laughed.

Ethan gave her his comical evil glare, before reaching down to grab a handful of snow and launching his own missile back in her direction. This was his idea of fun. He was soon fully immersed in the frolics, making friends as he went. Back upstairs Abi and Jack were starting to stir.

Abi looked across to the bunk bed and noticed Ethan was missing.

'Eth?' she said, hoping that he was hidden under his blanket.

'Jack, where's Ethan?' she asked.

Jack was barely awake, he leant over the top bunk to look down below. In his tiredness he misjudged his angle and came tumbling down to the floor in a heap. Abi laughed, even though she was concerned as to Ethan's whereabouts, that fall was worthy of a chuckle.

'I'm fine Abs don't worry,' said Jack trying to hide his embarrassment.

Jack himself then heard the noise coming from outside and looked at Abi knowingly. With that he made his way over to the window where he saw what he had suspected, Ethan soaked to the skin and running around the square indulging in horseplay.

Abi sat up and watched as her younger brother was having the time of his life. Jack started to get dressed, he wasn't about to let Ethan have all the fun. Within a matter of minutes he was out the front door and tackling his brother to the floor. Abi wasn't quite as keen to get involved so she had a quick shower and then got dressed and made her way downstairs into the sitting room.

'Breakfast?' asked Sue as she popped her head round the corner from the kitchen.

'That would be lovely,' replied Abi.

Sue had already asked the boys and once the food was ready she asked Abi to call them in. Both boys we're soaked so they stripped off their outer layer and placed them on the nearest radiator to dry. The boys were famished and ate everything Sue put in front of them. They had been living off their packs for quite a few days now and were consequently grateful for some home-cooked food. This breakfast, along with last night's meal, was exactly what the doctor ordered.

'Is Bernard working?' asked Jack.

'No, he's just off checking on the factory for half an hour,' replied Sue.

Sue explained how Bernard was the head elf in Santa's village and the running of the factory was his responsibility. He had agreed to give the children a tour this morning so was just making sure things were running smoothly before showing them around.

'I suggest you boys have a quick shower and perhaps a change of clothes,' said Sue. Abi was already dressed appropriately and was ready to go, but Sue was right, the boys needed to change. Abi asked Ethan to give her his tablet while the boys were getting ready. She was sitting down in the lounge surfing the internet, waiting for the boys when Sue joined her from the kitchen.

'You kids and the internet,' she said looking at Abi with her head almost buried in the screen.

'Oh sorry, I didn't see you there,' said Abi, aware that she could almost be seen as being rude if she continued to surf, after all she was a guest and needed to act appropriately.

'So, how long have you lived here?' asked Abi.

'Oh, longer than I can remember,' said Sue. What a strange answer Abi thought, unaware that Sue was actually being brutally honest.

'Does Santa live here?' the second those words left Abi's mouth she regretted asking.

'Not anymore,' replied Sue. 'I wonder where Bernard has got to?' she added quickly, desperately trying to change the subject.

Abi clearly had touched a nerve and didn't want to push the subject. There was a bit of an awkward silence for a minute or so before Jack came downstairs to join them, quickly followed by Ethan, his hair still soaking from the shower.

'You need to dry that,' said Abi pointing to Ethan's hair, 'you'll catch your death,' she added, realising that she sounded like her mother. He trotted back upstairs to finish drying his hair. Just then Bernard returned home.

'Morning everyone,' he said. 'What a lovely day it is out there.' The children got the impression that the weather was pretty much the same everyday here, so couldn't quite understand why Bernard was so jolly, although they had the feeling that everyone here was always so happy and full of joy.

'Right, it's now almost ten,' he said. 'Are you guys ready for a look around?'

'We're just waiting for Ethan,' said Jack, and with that Ethan came back down the stairs looking much more ready to leave.

'Right on cue young man,' laughed Sue.

The children all put their coats on and followed Bernard outside.

'Just a second,' he said as he popped back in to say goodbye to Sue. Abi could see them talking through the window. Sue kept referring to her watch, perhaps she was discussing what time lunch would be ready thought Abi, how wrong she was.

'OK, lets go,' said Bernard as he returned to the children.

'Where's Max?' he asked.

The dog had been asleep all morning and was not interested in moving, clearly the trip had taken much more out of him than the children realised, but they were happy to let him rest up today.

'Where are we going first?' asked Ethan as he walked alongside Bernard, keen to be first to see everything.

'We'll start with the village hall, then the factory, then if we have time the warehouse,' replied Bernard, clearly he had their morning mapped out. The village hall was not very far away at all, just across the square beyond the clock tower. The hall had a couple of steps up to the double entrance door. It was a tall, single-storey building and as with all the town's buildings it was impeccably decorated.

Bernard pushed open the double front doors. Even though he was an elf and barely over four feet tall, he had incredible strength and opened the doors effortlessly. Inside the hall was a huge spruce tree decorated with tinsel, baubles and various objects and lit with fairy lights. The hall was clearly used for gatherings and had a set of concertina chairs fixed to one wall, like you find in modern secondary schools these days.

There was also a stage on the opposite side, clearly designed for performances of one sort or another.

'Not a lot to see here really,' said Bernard. 'This is where we hold all our functions, and most importantly keep our Christmas tree,' he added, beaming with pride at the sight of the tree. The children could see a variety of pictures on the far wall, pictures it seemed of Santa Claus, and what looked like reindeers, but they weren't really close enough to see. Abi started to head over to take a closer look.

'Right let's go to the factory,' said Bernard.

Abi didn't quite get close enough to take a look before she had to turn round to follow the others. Bernard led them outside and down the steps.

'Aren't you going to lock up?' asked Jack.

'No need for locks around here,' he laughed. Clearly he was right, this village was so safe and secure and everyone knew everyone else.

'To the factory, you'll love this place Ethan,' he said as he led them back past his own home and towards a large building where many of the elves had been heading the night before. They entered the building through a side door and a narrow staircase led them upstairs. Abi and Jack were behind Ethan and Bernard. When Ethan reached the top of the stairs he stopped in his tracks.

'Wow!' he said before rushing forward onto a balcony of sorts. Jack and Abi quickly followed. Down below them was a magnificent workshop with hundreds, if not thousands, of elves beavering away manufacturing such a huge variety of toys. There was technology, games, sporting equipment, cuddly toys, basically you name it, they were making it.

The speed at which things were moving in this place was incredible, each and every elf knew their place and the whole workshop seemed to be running like clockwork. It was difficult for the naked eye to keep up with the production, one item would start from nothing and within seconds would be assembled and ready for use.

'But how...?' said Ethan as he watched numerous items being made.

'We've been doing this a long time,' said Bernard attempting to justify their skills.

'This is factory number seven,' he added. 'All thirty of them are pretty good at what they do by now.'

'Thirty! But you must make...' said Jack trying to figure out how many toys could be made in these thirty factories.

'A lot,' replied Bernard. 'We make a lot of toys.'

The three children were mesmerised by the workshop, clearly there were powers other than hard work afoot here. These elves themselves were other-worldly and the processes they applied in this factory were no less magical.

Abi was deep in thought as to what she had heard the day before.

'But if you make all these every year and no one delivers them, then where do they go?' she asked Bernard.

'The warehouses,' he replied, 'and that's where we're off to next.'

'But why bother?' asked Abi, clearly confused as to the effort these elves put in.

'Why bother? Well, that's what we do, that's who we are,' he defended himself sternly. 'And if there is the slimmest of chances, the faintest of chances that one day we'll be able to deliver again, then we must, we must be ready,' he added firmly. 'Now let me show you just what we're capable of.'

He led the children away from the balcony, although Ethan almost had to be peeled off the railing. They headed back downstairs and out into the village. They walked away from the square and towards the perimeter wall that surrounded the town. One part of the wall stood at the base of a large hill; there was a gap in this part of the wall and a large double door filled the void. It didn't look quite right, the door was in the rock face of the large hill. Bernard knocked on the door this time rather than opening it himself and four small elves pushed the doors outwards towards the village, the children followed Bernard inside.

It was slightly darker inside than usual and it took the children's eyes a few seconds to adjust to the light. When they finally managed to focus on what they were looking at they could almost not believe what they were seeing. They were standing in a huge warehouse with shelves reaching up above them into the darkness and isles as far as the eye could see. This was like the biggest Toys 'r' us store you could ever imagine. Ethan started to wander forward trying to see to the far end, but it was impossible, it stretched for such a long way. How many toys could be in here?

'There are toys here from the last twenty-four years,' announced Bernard. 'Some your parents would know and some you may be more familiar with.'

The children were in shock. They could never have imagined such a store, such a crazy village, with unimaginable factories and this epic warehouse.

'This is incredible,' said Jack.

'I don't know what to think,' added Abi.

Bernard just chuckled, this was the norm to him, but he could see how shocked and stunned the children were. It was now approaching midday and he had made a promise to Sue that they'd be back by then so he instructed the children to follow him back outside. He thanked the elves who had opened the door and told them to keep up the good work, before leading the children back across town to his cottage.

CHAPTER 21
An Introduction

SUNDAY, 22ND DECEMBER

Back at the cottage, Sue was putting the finishing touches to the lunch she had been preparing for the last half hour or so. Bernard was first in.

'Hi dear,' he said. 'I told you I'd have them back for twelve.'

'Lunch will be ready in a short while children,' said Sue. 'Why don't you go up and change into something more comfortable? That poor old dog of yours must be worn out, he hasn't stirred since you left,' she added giggling to herself.

Ethan was first to sprint upstairs and ran straight into the bedroom jumping on Abi's bed where Max was curled up still fast asleep. The poor dog was lifted from the mattress as Ethan bounced playfully on one end of the bed.

'Eth!' said Jack. 'Poor Max was trying to rest.'

Ethan settled down pretty quickly and gave his pet a hug. Max wasn't pleased at all as he crept off the bed crossing the room to curl up on the floor at the foot of the bunk bed.

'I bagsie the shower,' said Abi as she could see Jack trying to undress quickly.

'Aaarrggh!' said Jack, disappointed that his sister had outwitted him.

'Where's the tablet Eth?' he asked his brother as he looked for something to kill time while he waited for his turn in the shower.

Jack lay on the bottom bunk as he switched on the tablet to surf or perhaps play on an app or two. Ethan had climbed on the top bunk and was disappearing under the blanket with the Calendar. He was only under there about thirty seconds because he had forgotten that the glow the book had previously been emitting had stopped.

'Why did the book stop glowing?' he asked Jack as he leaned over to look at his brother.

Jack paused, not really sure if he was being honest, 'Perhaps it's found home? I don't really know Eth. Is there really no glow at all?'

Ethan opened the book. The first page was the instructions that they had received on the outset of this adventure and the map of their now distant home town. Then the amazing animation of Frozen Claw which Ethan would never tire of and then the message for Tiberius. The message for Fang followed that and then the forest scene, finally the instruction for the mysterious gate.

Jack noticed that another page was ready to turn, although the book was not glowing or appearing to be asking to be read. He turned the page. The boys waited, patiently, they exchanged glances; little by little a new message appeared.

'Abi!' shouted Ethan, before Jack managed to muffle the shout with his hand. Sue and Bernard could hear Ethan but suspected nothing but horseplay.

'Ssh,' said Jack pointing downstairs with his hand. Abi burst out of the shower wrapped in several towels. She could tell by the look on Jack's face that she was to be quiet. She crept over to the bunk bed on her tiptoes. About halfway across the room she realised that the boys were giving her the strangest look. She was almost comical in the way she was walking, there was no need to be quite so quiet and that dawned on her pretty quickly and she came the rest of the way normally.

'You clown Abi,' said Jack as Ethan giggled.

'Yeah, yeah, OK,' said Abi, she had very little defence for her comical actions.

The three of them looked at the book at what must be the final message appeared.

Thank you for returning this book intact. Santa Claus' Village is now reunited with its Advent Calendar. Santa Claus will be waiting to thank you for your efforts. A Merry Christmas to you all.

Abi noticed that the book had now developed a sort of live Calendar with date and time being displayed, as well as the weather conditions and a sort of countdown clock. The clock had a time in hours and minutes counting down, it read:

83 hours and 32 minutes

Jack looked at the time on his tablet, it was 12.28, he tried to make sense of the countdown as did Ethan and Abi.

'It's how long to go until Thursday,' said Ethan, his maths skills coming to the fore.

'And that's the 25th,' added Abi. 'Or what used to be Christmas Day.'

The one problem the children had was there had as yet been no sign of Santa Claus; was he even here? They had heard talk of him disappearing some time ago, or had he just retired here in his village? They needed to find out but how could they? Who could they ask?

The three of them stood there, deep in thought, a thousand and one things rushing through their minds. A call from downstairs broke the silence.

'Lunch is ready,' shouted Sue. 'Come and get it.'

Jack was the first one to go downstairs and into the kitchen to sit around the small dinner table. Sue had made a bit of a mixture, some sandwiches, scotch eggs, sausage rolls and other 'finger' foods. Jack dived in, he was never one to miss out on his food. Ethan, however, was a little fussy, picking his way through a few bits here and there. That just left Abi, who was a typical teenage girl, a little too diet-conscious for her own good.

'Bernard are you joining us?' asked Sue. He was sitting in the lounge watching the clock.

'I'll be through in a little while,' he replied.

The children had been eating for about ten minutes when they heard a gentle knock at the door. Bernard got up from the sofa and went to answer it. They could hear the sound of a lady at the door and her and Bernard were greeting each other. Bernard came through to the kids.

'There's someone next door who'd like to meet you kids,' he said.

The three of them looked at each other puzzled.

'Meet us?' asked Abi.

'That's right,' said Bernard. 'Sue told her of your visit and how nice and friendly you were and she asked if she could come and meet you. I hope that's OK?'

Jack shrugged his shoulders, 'Sure, why not.'

'Great!' said Bernard. 'Come through when you're ready.'

The children washed down their food with some of the juice Sue had provided, stood up, straightened their clothing and made their way through to the lounge.

Standing in front of the open fireplace was a tall lady – well at least in comparison to the elves – she was about five foot five or five foot six, of perfectly human proportion. She was dressed from head to toe in red and white, with a red shawl trimmed with white fur.

'Hello children,' she said. 'I'm Mrs Claus. But you can call me Jessica.'

The children were in shock, totally lost for words.

'Are you OK?' asked Mrs Claus, a little worried by the children's response. Still nothing, Mrs Claus looked at Sue for some kind of help.

'Sit down, sit down,' said Sue, ushering the children gently to the sofa.

'Mrs Claus means you no harm, she's just come to meet you,' she added.

Ethan whispered to Abi and then to Jack, he was trying to determine if they should ask about Santa. Abi nodded and gave Jack a nudge.

'Where's Santa?' asked Jack, blunt as ever.

Mrs Claus sat on the remaining armchair.

'I wish I knew,' she said. 'It's been over thirty years since we last saw him, thirty years…'

'So he's not here?' asked Abi.

'I'm sorry but no,' replied Mrs Claus.

'But…' hesitated Abi, looking at Jack and Ethan who nodded.

'But what?' asked Mrs Claus.

'But we have his book,' insisted Abi.

'His book?' asked Mrs Claus.

'Yes, his Calendar,' continued Abi.

Mrs Claus looked taken a back, she wasn't exactly sure if the children were making this up or if they even had the right Calendar. She was half expecting them to produce a basic everyday advent calendar, the sort children used to open on the days leading up to Christmas with chocolates or toys inside.

'Can I see it?' she asked.

Ethan bolted up the stairs falling over Max on the way up who had decided to come down to meet their visitor. Max trotted straight up to Mrs Claus and nuzzled her thigh with his head. She patted him gently.

'What a lovely dog. Is he yours?' she asked.

'Yes, he's come all the way here with us,' said Jack.

'Remarkable,' commented Mrs Claus as she looked at Bernard and Sue, shaking her head slightly in almost disbelief that these children had made such an epic journey.

Ethan came bounding down the stairs, missing the last two and stumbling into the back of the sofa. Jack sniggered. Red faced with embarrassment Ethan approached Mrs Claus and slowly handed her the Calendar.

She looked at the front of the Calendar, she was instantly in no doubt it was genuine. She clutched it to her chest emotionally and gave it a real hug. The children could see she was emotional.

'Are you OK?' asked Abi.

'Yes, yes, I'll be fine,' she replied, 'but thank you for asking.'

'Would you mind if I hang on to this?' she asked, referring to the book.

'I guess so,' replied Jack 'If Santa's not here, you're the next best thing I guess.' With that Abi game him a bit of a dig, she wasn't impressed by his lack of sentiment.

'Oh, that's OK,' said Mrs Claus to Abi, 'I suppose he's right.'

She stood up slowly.

'Now,' she said. 'I would love for you three to come and spend some time with me this afternoon and perhaps stay for dinner if that sounds OK?'

The three children looked at each other and seemed keen to take Mrs Claus up on her offer.

'Yes, of course,' said Abi.

Max whined pitifully at his apparent exclusion.

'And you of course,' said Mrs Claus as she bent over to pat the dog.

'Shall we say three o'clock,' she said. The children nodded in response. With that Mrs Claus said her goodbyes and left the cottage.

'Well, you've had quite some adventure,' said Bernard, 'and you are meeting all sorts of new people.'

'It's all a bit of a blur,' replied Abi. 'I'm half expecting to wake up at any time.'

'Well, I can assure you that Sue and I are as real as the moon and the stars,' replied Bernard. With that he asked the children if they'd like a hot chocolate, the answer was obvious and he rushed off to the kitchen to make them a drink. Sue stayed with the children in the lounge and put on some classic Christmas songs for them to listen to.

This was the first time the children had heard such songs and they really did take some getting used to. Bernard soon returned with his drinks and the five of them and Max sat peacefully drinking and sharing stories of the children's journey so far.

Sue and Bernard could hardly believe what the children had endured. Bernard was particularly happy to hear how Rudolph had come to their aid.

'He's a good lad old Rudy,' he said. 'Do you want to meet the others?'

'Others?' asked Ethan excitedly.

'Oh, yes there are plenty of others!' said Bernard, clearly enticing the children.

Ethan was a keen as mustard, the other two were also quite happy to go and see what Bernard was talking about so they collected their coats and prepared to leave.

'I'm coming this time,' said Sue slipping on her jacket.

'I love your boots,' said Abi as she watched Sue slip on her fur-lined boots

'Oh, these old things, Bernard made these for me last year,' she said, clearly proud of her boots but wanting to remain modest.

The small group went out and Max followed. They headed behind the cottage and down a relatively steep path towards a large barn of sorts. Approaching the barn the children started to pick up the scent of wildlife, some sort of cattle or perhaps horses thought Abi; they could hear some strange grunts and groans coming from inside. Alongside the barn were several large bails of what could only have been hay and a large pitchfork.

'Grab what you can kids,' said Bernard pointing at the hay.

The children duly obliged. Max had started to drift towards the back of the group, he wasn't sure what they were about to encounter and didn't have the confidence of the children. Arms filled with hay, they turned to the front of the barn and could see that one side of the barn door was open. Bernard disappeared inside. The children stopped.

'Go on,' said Sue. 'Follow Bernard, it's safe enough.'

Ethan went first followed by Jack, with Abi accompanying Sue. Max crept slowly after the last of them. Inside was well lit with the most amazing herd of reindeer. They were all glad of the hay and Ethan did not hesitate in hand feeding the caribou.

Jack soon followed, he was an animal lover, but not quite as enthusiastic as Ethan. Abi was a little slower to engage, she was a little bit intimidated by the sheer size of the reindeer.

'These are amazing,' said Ethan. 'Can they do what the other one can?'

he asked, clearly referring to Rudolph's special ability.

'Most can,' replied Bernard, 'but this fellow is a little bit young,' he added patting one of the smaller reindeer on the snout. 'It's been quite some time though since any of them took to the air.'

'Why's that?' asked Abi.

'Not that certain, but it was long ago,' explained Bernard. 'Santa took them out many years ago and he never returned. The reindeer returned a few at a time, a couple of them had some minor injuries,' he continued. 'Rudolph, the reindeer you met in the forest has never set foot back in the village, he roams the forest like a lost soul.'

The mood in the barn had changed slightly and the children felt a real sense of sadness for the first time since they entered the village. Mrs Claus was visibly emotional when she held the Calendar, but these animals were like Bernard's children and Rudolph was obviously close to his heart.

The time in the barn passed quickly, Max had grown in confidence and the reindeer barely noticed him there. Suddenly one of the larger bull reindeer sneezed loudly, one of the bits of hay had tickled his nose as he chewed vigorously. Max almost leapt out of his skin, he shot out of the barn and a few seconds passed by before his head returned around the door, looking to see if the coast was clear.

'Ha, ha, Max,' said Jack. 'You need to learn to toughen up mate!' Max was always dependable to lift people's spirits with his unintentional humour.

The children had spent a good hour in the barn, with the exception of Bernard's emotional tales, the atmosphere was lovely and the reindeer didn't seem to tire of their company at all. When it was time to leave Bernard did a quick check of the reindeer one by one making sure they were well stocked with food and drink before suggesting to the children they should head back.

'Right, off we go then, you'll need to wash up before heading round to Mrs Claus,' he said. The children had almost lost all sense of where they were in that last hour and the excitement of visiting Mrs Claus' home started to fill their thoughts.

They quickly made their way back to the cottage. This time Jack and Ethan took showers while Abi just changed her clothes and washed away the scent of the reindeer. Abi had a feeling that their quest was coming to an end. She was now starting to long to see her parents once again, this prompted her to send her mother and father a text, once again reassuring them of their safety, but this time suggesting a return in the near future, the message read:

> *Hi Mum, hi Dad, sorry I can't phone but I'm just sending this to tell you we're warm and sheltered. We've met some friends and hopefully we'll be on our way back soon. We all love you both and can't wait to be home. Will txt soon.* ☺

Jack came downstairs first to join Abi and before long Ethan too. It was now just after half past two and they would soon be heading for an afternoon with Mrs Claus.

CHAPTER 22
Mrs Claus

SUNDAY, 22ND DECEMBER

Bernard sent the children off unaccompanied to Mrs Claus' house, the directions were straightforward and even though the afternoon light was fading the village was easy to navigate and there were plenty of helpful elves nearby.

The children made their way slowly across the square still taking in all of their surroundings in the wonderfully festive village.

'This place is amazing,' said Abi.

'Imagine living here all year,' added Ethan.

'That would suit you shorty!' replied Jack. The village almost suited Ethan down to the ground, although that wouldn't last forever.

'Don't be mean Jack,' responded Abi. 'You're hardly a giant and you'd have been a perfect fit yourself just a couple of years ago.'

Jack just chuckled to himself, Ethan was generally at the butt of all his jokes, but Ethan usually gave as good as he got.

The children walked past the village hall and stopped outside a larger than average house.

'This must be it,' said Abi.

Mrs Claus was what Ethan had described earlier as 'full size', not like the elves that inhabited the village, and consequently her house was bigger than the cottage the children had been residing at. Her house itself was relatively modest, but was beautifully decorated with a myriad of lights and numerous hand-carved festive artefacts. There were about half a dozen steps up to a large porch which had a hammock covered in blankets hanging to the left of the front door.

The three children made their way up the stairs and Jack knocked the door gently. They only had to wait a few seconds before Mrs Claus answered.

'Hello you three,' she said as she opened the door.

'Please, come in,' she added.

The children walked in to her hallway. It had a wide staircase leading up to the second floor and what must have been the sleeping quarters. To the left there was a door which, judging by the smell, led to the kitchen. To their right was an open door to what the children assumed must be the lounge.

'Can I take you coats?' asked Mrs Claus holding out her arms. The children took off their outdoor coats and gave them to Mrs Claus who placed them one by one on the coat rack alongside the front door.

'Thank you,' said Ethan politely as she hung up his coat, he was desperate to make a good impression.

'You're welcome,' she replied. 'Now come through to the lounge, we'll have a chat before I serve up food a little later.'

The children followed her though to her lounge which had an open fireplace with several logs burning brightly. The outside light was fading fast and this beautifully lit living room was so cosy and welcoming. The children all sat together on a large sofa to the side of the fireplace. Mrs Claus took one of the two remaining comfortable armchairs.

'Well, it's truly amazing what you three, or I thought it was four?' she said looking around for Max.

'Oh, he's curled up on the bunk bed at Bernard and Sue's,' explained Jack.

'Oh, I see, well either way it's amazing what a journey you've made. Whatever possessed you to come so far from your home?' she asked

There was a slight delay as the children paused for thought, what indeed had inspired them to commit to such a huge adventure.

'Not sure really,' started Jack. 'But that book is like nothing we have ever seen, and once we knew it was something to do with Christmas, after speaking to the older folk in the village we knew it must be pretty important.'

'So what did the people tell you about Christmas?' she asked

'Lots of different versions,' said Abi. 'There are so many different stories, mostly really happy ones, but they all agreed how sad it was when it all stopped.'

'Why did it stop?' asked Ethan looking at Mrs Claus for some explanation.

Mrs Claus looked uncertain as to how to answer this.

'If I'm honest I'm not sure myself,' she said. 'You've followed instructions in the Calendar to return it here to Santa, but that's just the problem, he's not here and hasn't been for many years. I suppose that's the reason Christmas stopped, but as to the reason Santa disappeared, well that's just a mystery,' she concluded, turning to stare out of the window to her left.

Abi looked at the boys with a frown, clearly she felt they were prying too much into Mrs Claus' life and were upsetting her.

'We didn't mean to upset you,' she said to Mrs Claus.

'Oh, bless you dear, don't worry,' she replied. 'I've cried myself to sleep many a time, but that was some years ago now. It still hurts but we've all come to accept that Santa may never return.'

'Now how about a drink?' she asked.

'Hot chocolate!' Ethan yelped.

'Ethan!' Abi barked, a little embarrassed at his cheekiness.

'That's OK,' said Mrs Claus. 'So you're a fan of our special cocoa then?'

'We all are,' Jack said as he joined in the conversation. 'It's the best, well equal best chocolate we've ever had.'

'So someone else is after my title for best hot chocolate recipe!' said Mrs Claus mischievously.

She left the room for only a few minutes before returning with four large mugs of hot chocolate for the children and herself. The four of them sat drinking their cocoa in silence, the drink itself warranted their full attention and even Ethan was able to sit quietly enjoying his treat.

Once they had finished the drink, the children gave Mrs Claus a pretty in-depth recollection of their adventures. Jack was the main narrator, but Abi occasionally jumped in to correct him and Ethan repeated the parts he found most enjoyable, particularly Max's bravery in the whole Lupus Grimm saga.

Mrs Claus was truly amazed at their resilience and at the courage children of such tender ages had shown. The various characters along the trip were known to her and she was pleased to hear of Rudolph's wellbeing. Her face turned sour as the children explained about their problems with a certain Mr Grimm.

'That awful man,' she said, 'if my husband was here, he'd have cause to pay him a visit.' That was the first time the children had heard her refer to Santa Claus as her husband and it suddenly dawned on them what this poor lady had lost, it wasn't just some man in a suit who dedicated his life to helping children across the world, this was her husband, her soul mate, her life. They were glad they had at least been able to return the Calendar, even if it was a modest comfort to Mrs Claus.

After listening to the children's story enthusiastically, Mrs Claus suggested they headed through to the kitchen for some supper.

'Now, as you three have never enjoyed a Christmas dinner, that's exactly what we're going to have,' she declared. Jack's eyes lit up, he lived for his food and was keen to see what Christmas dinner entailed.

Mrs Claus had prepared the whole works, Turkey, cranberry, sausages wrapped in bacon, about a dozen vegetables, followed by a dark, rich Christmas pudding. The children sat down in anticipation.

'What are these?' asked Abi looking at the Christmas crackers that Mrs Claus had placed between each of the placemats.

'Those are crackers,' she answered. 'We'll pull them during our meal.'

That didn't mean an awful lot to the children, they really were absolutely lost on any of the traditions of Christmas.

'Jack could you do me a favour?' asked Mrs Claus as she carried the turkey over to the table. 'Could you fetch the carving knife and fork from the drawer on the dresser please?'

Jack walked over to the large, wooden dresser covered in a variety of ivy and holly wreaths, he opened the drawer and reached in to take out the items she required. He took both the carving knife and the fork out of the drawer and then noticed a small picture frame with a photo inside. He placed the items on the dresser and slowly lifted out the picture frame, he found the person in the picture strangely familiar.

Mrs Claus noticed him looking intently at the picture frame.

'Are you OK young man?' she asked. Jack looked up quickly.

'Er… yes…' he stuttered. 'Who's this?'

'Let me see,' she said reaching out so Jack could hand her the photo.

'Oh…' she said pausing clearly full of emotion, 'that's Santa, that's my Kris.'

'Kris?' asked Jack

'Why, yes, that's his name, Kris Kringle,' she replied.

Jack suddenly looked at Abi and Ethan with a sense of urgency.

'What is it Jack?' asked Abi.

Jack wasn't sure how to respond, he was conscious that he didn't want to upset Mrs Claus, but he had a feeling that what he was about to share with them would be life changing.

'Could Abi and Ethan see the picture?' he asked Mrs Claus gently.

'Why of course,' she replied. 'I have many more packed away, they used to be too painful to have around but you're welcome to take a look.' She handed the photo to Abi before leaving the room to retrieve her various photo albums.

Abi looked at the photo with Ethan, initially she just saw a picture of Santa, very much as she imagined, then she too saw what Jack and by now Ethan saw, 'Old Kris'.

'It can't be,' said Abi looking at a very animated Jack. The three of them could not believe what they were seeing, was the photo that clear? Was it definitely 'Old Kris'?

'It is though, it is,' replied Jack excitedly.

Ethan was looking somewhat confused, as he seemed to be trying to remember something.

'I said Kris,' he declared.

'What do you mean you said Kris?' asked Abi.

'I said Kris, then the gate opened,' he said referring back to the forest.

'What gate? Oh, that gate,' said Jack as he got up to speed with Ethan's thinking.

'We've got to be sure,' said Abi. 'We can't risk upsetting this poor lady.' The children were so excited, but were very aware of the pain that Mrs Claus had been through.

Mrs Claus returned with her collection of photos but insisted that they sat down for dinner first before they reminisced with her. Clearly she was unaware of what the children were suspecting, she too would be far more eager to investigate if she knew. The children sat down and started their supper, which as they soon discovered was one of the most amazing meals they had ever been served. Regardless of the quality of their feast, the children were almost unable to contain their excitement. Mrs Claus made sure the children had all they wanted and then proceeded to serve up the most delicious Christmas pudding, a desert the children had never had the pleasure of trying before.

'This is amazing,' said Jack, his compliment was greeted by a smile from Mrs Claus.

'Why thank you,' she responded, 'it's one of my specialities.'

Once the children were well fed Mrs Claus led them back to the living room where she had prepared some mince pies as a snack. The three children were almost fit to burst, even the usual conservative Abi.

'Mrs Claus...' started Ethan.

'Please, call me Jessica,' she replied.

'Er, Jessica, could we see more pictures of Santa?' he asked.

'Oh, yes, of course,' she replied. 'I almost forgot.'

She then took hold of several albums that she had fetched earlier and handed one to Abi and another for Jack and Ethan to share. The children opened the albums and were quickly turning page after page, to the confusion of Mrs Claus. After a minute or so Jack leant over and whispered to Abi, now this wasn't normally how the children would act as whispering could often be seen as rude, but that was the last thing on their minds.

'What is it dear?' asked Mrs Claus, clearly aware that the children were not acting particularly rationally.

The children all looked at Mrs Claus and then at each other, there was a long and awkward silence.

'Well?' she added, still perfectly patient.

Jack decided he had to make the first move.

'It's hard to say,' he started. 'We can't be one hundred per cent certain, but it all seems to fit.'

'Well, I'm all ears,' she said with a little giggle, unaware of the gravity of the situation.

'It's about Santa or Kris I suppose, or both,' he stuttered, 'not really sure where to begin.'

'Santa or Kris?' she said clearly confused. 'Well, Santa is Kris sweetheart.'

'Well, that's what we think isn't it Abs?' responded Jack as he passed the buck onto his sister.

Abi was far more direct, far more straight to the point.

'We think Old Kris is Santa,' she declared.

Mrs Claus sat up slightly in her chair, she could feel that the children were uncomfortable and was starting to worry a little.

'Old Kris?' she asked.

'Yes,' replied Abi. 'Old Kris from our hometown is Santa, or at least that's what we think,' she added pointing at the photos in the album.

Mrs Claus seemed to take a few seconds to digest what Abi was saying, she was still not entirely sure what the children were talking about.

'I don't quite understand,' she said.

Abi seemed to realise how obscure they were sounding, she tried to make what they were saying more succinct.

'There's an old guy in our hometown called Kris,' she explained. 'He's the spitting image of Santa, I mean he looks identical.'

Mrs Claus was now perched on the front of her seat.

'Go on,' she directed Abi.

'Well, he's been living there for twenty or thirty years, he was in the accident on the pass years ago,' explained Abi.

'And his cocoa is just like yours!' joined in Ethan.

'Accident?' asked Mrs Claus.

'Yes, there was a big crash up on the pass in the winter years ago,' said Jack, 'and lots of people were injured.'

Mrs Claus was trying to make sense of all this information she was being given, after all these years. Was her long lost husband just that, lost? She had previously been given false hope or sightings on various occasions, but it was a long time since she had heard anything at all.

She sat pensively, trying to make sense of this news and trying to decide how to act. The children all sat to full attention, eyes wide and pulses racing.

Amazingly Mrs Claus responded in the calmest possible manner.

'OK, this is what we're going to do,' she said. 'We're going to speak to Bernard and tell him what it is you think you know.' She wasn't trying to dismiss them or their information but wanted it analysed rationally. She ushered the children through to the hallway and handed them their coats, the party then headed off back to Bernard and Sue's.

CHAPTER 23
Putting the Pieces Together

SUNDAY, 22ND DECEMBER

Bernard and Sue were sitting peacefully in their lounge. Sue was knitting yet another Christmas jumper for her husband and Bernard was nose-deep in a book, predictably a Christmas novel. Mrs Claus knocked the door calling out, 'Sue, Bernard are you there?'

Sue got up and made her way to the door, she opened it to greet them.

'Hello, you're back a bit earlier than we expected?' she said, clearly puzzled at their early return.

'Hi Sue, sorry to disturb you, is Bernard with you?' asked Mrs Claus.

'Why of course,' replied Sue. 'Come in, come in.'

Mrs Claus and the children made their way into the lounge where Bernard was waiting for them.

'Hello,' he said standing up. 'Let Sue take your coats.'

Sue took their coats. The three children all sat down on the sofa as Mrs Claus stood in front of the fire, pacing from side to side slowly. This information had her a little rattled, this wasn't the first time she had been offered hope but it was a long time since the last false dawn, and there was something different about the children's story.

Mrs Claus explained to Bernard and Sue what the children had told her, occasionally handing over to the children for them to fill in the blanks. Their hosts were as confused as Mrs Claus, they too had heard many tales of sightings over the many years since Santa's disappearance but this was from such an unexpected source. The combination of the children's adventure, the return of the Advent Calendar and the children being convinced of the link between 'Old Kris' and Santa, stirred something in Mrs Claus and both Sue and Bernard.

'Tell me again where you live,' said Bernard to the children.

'In Willow Cove, in the UK,' replied Abi.

'And that's where you found the Calendar? And that's where your friend

Kris lives?' Bernard said as he continued with his questioning.

'He's not really our friend, but yes he's from Willow Cove too,' replied Jack.

Bernard sat back in his chair and thought to himself for a few seconds. He looked at his watch and turned to Mrs Claus.

'Could I speak to you in the hall for a minute?' he asked.

'Of course Bernard,' she replied and they both made their way out into the hallway. The children and Sue sat patiently in the lounge waiting for their return, which didn't take that long at all.

Mrs Claus walked back over to the fireplace and Bernard followed her in. The children noticed that he now had his coat in his hand.

'I'm just heading out for a while,' he said. 'I'm going to see Patrick, one of the elves that used to help with the navigation back in the day.'

'OK darling,' replied Sue. 'I'll put a drink on while we wait for you.'

The children were quite happy to sit in the lounge, particularly as Sue had suggested that another hot chocolate was imminent. Ethan got up and headed upstairs to check on Max, he'd been relatively quiet for the last couple of days and Ethan was a little worried.

Max was resting peacefully on the bottom bunk when Ethan entered the room. He lifted his head to acknowledge his friend, but that was all, he was making the most of his rest. Ethan tilted his head back and rolled his eyes, no one needed that much rest surely he thought. He headed over to the bedroom window to look out over the square. He noticed Bernard deep in conversation with four or five elves, two of them then rushed off to their cottages. Ethan suspected that news of their revelation was starting to spread throughout the village. Clearly this would be life changing for the locals, but Ethan worried that perhaps they might be mistaken about old Kris.

He ran downstairs and yelled, 'What if we're wrong! We might have got it all wrong.'

Mrs Claus' face changed slightly, was this new hope being taken away before they had a chance to investigate?

'We're not,' declared Abi. 'It's him, I'm sure of it.'

Mrs Claus didn't want poor Ethan to carry such a burden and was quick to put his mind at ease.

'Don't worry young man,' she said. 'We'll look into everything properly, nobody is to blame for anything here, don't you worry at all.' The noise of the kettle whistled through from the kitchen and Sue was quick to pop out of her chair and head off to make their drinks.

Bernard had just arrived at Patrick's cottage. He knocked on the door and waited.

'Hello Bernard,' said Patrick, popping his head out of the window to the side of the front door. 'Come round the back, the locks jammed,' he added pointing at the front door. Bernard made his way around the back of the cottage and entered though the back door. Patrick lived alone in the cottage and his home was really in need of a little attention. Patrick was somewhat of a hoarder, lots of technology and parts all over the place.

'How's things Bernard, what can I do for you?' he asked.

'I was hoping you were back in from the factory,' replied Bernard. 'It's a strange one really, I need you to come with me up to the Nav Centre to check something out.'

'The Nav Centre?' asked Patrick. 'I haven't been up there for a week or two.'

The Nav or Navigation Centre used to be the centre of operations when Santa used to complete his Christmas deliveries over thirty years ago. Patrick virtually ran the whole operation, he was a technological genius and made light of all the logistics involved. It was perhaps his dedication to the job that kept him from finding a girlfriend all those years. He kept a keen eye on the centre and regularly visited it to keep it tidy, unlike his poor cottage.

The two of them went up towards the warehouse the children had visited earlier, but turned off to the left as they approached the hill that seemed to house the warehouse. They walked up a small path that wound around like an old fashioned helter skelter. At the top stood an impressive circular building, very modern looking with numerous satellite dishes situated on its flat roof and a full three hundred and sixty degree balcony surrounding it.

'Here we are,' said Patrick proudly, this clearly was his second home.

He opened up the metallic doors and ushered Bernard in before following himself. Patrick switched the light on and the whole room lit up instantly. There were multiple computers situated throughout the room all with radar monitors alongside. In the centre of the room was a white, circular table that Patrick ducked underneath to switch on. The table immediately changed into a form of touch screen display with a map of the entire planet on it.

'Still impressive, eh?' said Patrick proudly as he looked at the table.

'Your greatest creation yet,' replied Bernard. 'You really used to do your thing up here.' Patrick was somewhat of a genius, his fellow elves used to be in awe of his abilities and it had been such a waste of his abilities these last three decades or so since Santa's absence.

'So what's the story Bernard?' asked Patrick.

'It's kind of another sighting,' he replied, to which Patrick tutted.

'But I think this one's a little different,' added Bernard.

'Well, I haven't heard that before,' replied Patrick sarcastically.

'No really, we've even got the Calendar back this time,' Bernard pointed out.

'The Calendar? Really?' replied a clearly excited Patrick. 'But how? Who?' he added slightly unnerved by what he had just learnt.

'The children that arrived yesterday came with it, they followed the instructions you laid out,' explained Bernard.

'Did they tell you where they found it?' and Bernard nodded.

'Let's take a look then,' said Patrick as he ran his hands across the large touch screen. The map showed Santa's route on his trip in fine detail and stored the information for year after year, quite remarkable technology for thirty years ago. Patrick looked at the system and went back to 20th December 1979 when Santa was last heard of. He had been performing a trial run as he did every year and was last contacted whilst over Shropshire in England.

'This was the last contact,' said Patrick as he pointed to the West Midlands county of Shropshire. Bernard looked over the map, but was unsure as to where exactly the children lived.

'Show me where Willow Cove is?' he said to Patrick, who duly typed in the village name to locate it on the map. The village lit up with a blue light.

'Now show me exactly where we last had contact with Santa,' he instructed Patrick.

Patrick turned his attention back to the map and selected several options on the map, attempting to illustrate the exact point of their last contact all those years ago.

'There we are,' said Patrick as the green light on the map clearly showed the exact location of Santa's last transmission. It was quite obvious that this was only about one hundred miles as the crow flies from the village of Willow Cove where the children had travelled from.

They both took a step back from the map, pausing for a few seconds, then returned to take an even closer look at the image. They were hovering over the map when they turned to each other.

'That's pretty close, don't you think?' said Patrick.

'Closer than any of the others,' replied Bernard, clearly referring to the previous sightings they had been given over the years.

They turned back to the map. There was a pause of only a minute or two as they both looked closer at the locations they were studying, before Patrick spoke.

'I think you'd best ready the reindeer,' he said. 'I think you've got a journey to make.' Patrick nodded knowingly at Bernard. He instructed Patrick to stay in the control tower and to plot a route for him before he left to share his news with the others.

CHAPTER 24
Prepare the Herd

SUNDAY, 22ND DECEMBER

Bernard returned to the house as quickly as possible, he came in through the front door and hung his coat on the rack before making his way into the lounge. The children were all in hysterics and Sue and Mrs Claus were almost doubled over with laughter.

'What's so funny?' asked Bernard trying to share in the joke.

'Just telling them about that time you had a little too much mulled wine and I found you in the barn,' she said. Bernard had a sudden flashback to the time he woke up in the barn after a rather heavy night out. The image of him snuggled up with a dozen wild reindeer wearing nothing but his festive socks was one which would bring laughter to any room.

'Well, Bernard, I'll never be able to look at you the same way again,' declared Mrs Claus. Bernard went bright red, clearly embarrassed by Sue's story.

'Thanks darling,' he said to his wife sarcastically.

'Sorry dear,' she replied, 'but you must admit it's the best story.'

Bernard walked over to the fireplace to warm his hands. Mrs Claus was keen to find out what his investigation had led to.

'Well, did you speak to Patrick?' she asked.

'Yes,' he replied, 'I did, and the children may have a case.'

Mrs Claus sat forward in her chair. Bernard explained to the children who Patrick was and then addressed the whole group as he relayed what he and Patrick had looked into and what they had discovered. The locations were barely thirty minutes or so apart, taking the aerial route that is. The close proximity of Willow Cove to Santa's last known location certainly added credibility to what the children suspected.

Bernard and everyone else in the village had been given so much hope previously with numerous sightings, he explained to the children that they had spent years investigating these sightings from as far afield as Australia,

New Zealand, from Russia to Africa, no continent had been without sightings. This, however, was the first time they had received news from somewhere quite so credible.

'So, if it is fine with you, I'd like to take the boys out and look into it,' Bernard said to Mrs Claus.

Mrs Claus took quite some time to respond. The children couldn't quite understand why she wouldn't want Bernard to head off to investigate. He had done this many times and taken another couple of elves with him to help, the reason for her delay though soon became apparent.

'Yes, Bernard, you shall go and I'm coming with you,' she insisted.

Bernard looked at Sue in shock. Was Mrs Claus really going to travel all that way with him? She had never travelled with the reindeer before, this would be an absolute first. He did, however, fully understand that this was her decision and her decision alone.

'If you're sure that's what you want, then that's what we'll do,' said a surprised Bernard, but Mrs Claus had another shock in store.

'And Abi is coming with us,' she added.

Abi's face changed. The three children had all been sitting with grins as wide as the Cheshire cat's across their faces, either because they felt pleased with themselves at their potential discovery of Santa or because they could feel hope filling the hearts of their hosts; but now they looked concerned. Abi was clearly unsure if this was something she was ready for, whereas the boys were gutted that they wouldn't be travelling with them.

'Don't worry Abi,' said Mrs Claus, 'it's perfectly safe.' Her and Bernard may have had full confidence in the reindeer, but wasn't this the exact journey that led to Santa's disappearance thought Abi.

'And don't you worry either boys,' said Bernard, 'you'll get your turn.' Clearly he understood that their faces were not full of fear but full of disappointment.

Bernard decided that they would head off at first light so they had the rest of the evening and into the night to plan their journey. He explained that the boys would head up to the control tower with Sue so that they could monitor the journey with Patrick. The boys looked at each other eagerly, this wasn't their first choice but it was a great alternative. It meant they would get to take a look at all the cool gadgets that Bernard had explained that Patrick had.

'I suggest that we all get an early night tonight,' said Mrs Claus. 'Bernard will get some help from Patrick and the others and they will get everything ready for us.'

'That's right,' responded Patrick. 'I'll make a few calls and set things in motion. Abi, you'd best get as much rest as you can, you're in for a real treat tomorrow and you wouldn't want to miss a thing.'

Abi, however, was going to find sleep hard to come by that evening, she was stepping into the unknown and, with the exception of this whole adventure, was rarely one to take risks. Mrs Claus and Bernard though felt that she was the right choice of the three children to accompany them and they needed a little help pinpointing the exact location of 'Old Kris'.

After half an hour or so Mrs Claus said her goodbyes for the evening and together with Bernard she left, leaving the children in the safe hands of Sue. Abi decided she was going to try and get a very early night; it was already dark so she hoped she could get some much needed sleep. The two boys, however, were quite happy to stay in the lounge sharing Ethan's tablet to keep them entertained.

Bernard paid a visit to the barn to ensure the reindeer would be ready for the following morning. He also had to make sure the sled was prepared, it had been over twenty years since they had last flown. The sled was in immaculate condition; but not quite as grand as Santa's original sled which the children had uncovered in the cave back in Willow Cove, but still a real piece of engineering mastery. The elves were able to create magnificent items and this sled was no exception. Bernard made sure he was thorough with his inspection and then returned to the village hall where he and Mrs Claus had asked a few of the more senior elves to gather.

The elves had heard a few murmurings of what was underfoot and Mrs Claus wanted to explain exactly what was going on. She led the elves into the village hall before asking them to sit down and listen to what she had to say. She took to the small stage to the left of the hall.

'It's been quite a long time since I've called a meeting like this,' she started, 'but some information has come to light that suggests – and I must insist that it does only suggest – that Santa has been sighted.'

A buzz of excitement filled the room, the elves were noticeably animated and were all questioning each other, hoping beyond hope that their long lost leader had indeed been discovered.

'Okay, okay, settle down, settle down,' she asked. 'Bernard is taking the sleigh out to find out more, but this time I'm going with him.'

There was a brief silence. The elves were somewhat shocked, they knew that if Mrs Claus was taking to the air that this 'sighting' carried more weight than any before. Several elves were huddled in a small group discussing something intently, Mrs Claus looked over to the group.

'Is there something you need to share with us?' she asked.

One of the older looking elves spoke. 'If this sighting is genuine and if you do find him, why hasn't he come back before?' he asked, while the others in the group nodded.

Mrs Claus had asked herself this question many times, but her faith in her husband did not waver.

'Well, that's what I'm hoping to find out,' she replied. 'If there was a way he could have returned then I'm absolutely certain he would have.' The confidence in her voice was obvious and the elves that had asked the question could sense this and were buoyed by her strength.

'Yes, yes I'm sure you're right,' a few of them said simultaneously.

'Now, if there's nothing further I need to prepare for the journey,' she said as she stepped down from the stage. The elves all wished her good look and hoped she would have a successful trip. Bernard came through the main entrance and ensured Mrs Claus that the sleigh was ready and that the reindeer had been prepared. He could feel the electricity in the air in the hall, clearly the elves had taken well to Mrs Claus' news. The village itself would soon be full of hope and a newfound purpose.

One of the elves beckoned Bernard over. 'What is it Arthur?' asked Bernard.

'Hi Bernard,' he replied. 'It's just that a few of us were wondering what would happen if he did return? It's now the 21st and Christmas Eve will soon be upon us,' he added.

Bernard paused for thought, what in fact was going to happen? He was certain that everything would work out.

'Well, the factory is on schedule, as it has been every year, so everything here is in place,' he said. 'Patrick has the Nav Centre prepared as he always does, so we'll just have to wait and see how things pan out.'

His confidence comforted the other elves. Were they finally going to get to spread their Christmas cheer once again? Surely time was against them.

Bernard left the elves to their thoughts and made his way out of the hall and back across the square home. Sue had prepared him a nice warm drink and he sat down in the lounge with the boys for a chat.

'I hope you two will be able to help Patrick tomorrow?' he said. It was important to him that the boys felt involved, he realised they were disappointed at not making the journey and wanted them to feel part of this whole mission.

'We'll do anything we can to help,' said Jack. 'Anything at all.'

'Good,' replied Bernard. 'Now I know its early but I suggest we get a good night's sleep as tomorrow will be an early start and a very very long day.'

The boys finished their drinks and made their way upstairs. Abi had actually managed to drop off so the boys tiptoed their way across the room to their bunks. Something in the window caught Jack's eye and he headed over before beckoning Ethan to come and look at what he had seen. The square was almost full of elves, all of whom were very animated. Some were hugging each other, others were shaking hands vigorously and some even high-fiving each other repeatedly. It was obvious that they had heard of the plans that were underfoot and the boys suddenly felt very pressured, after all it was their insistence that 'Old Kris' was Santa Claus that had led to this excitement. They both returned to the bunk beds for their night's sleep. Jack slipped into the bottom bunk, nudging Max to the side. The bed wasn't particularly spacious as it was and Max's lump of a torso made Jack's night sleep more of a challenge. As the boys drifted off to sleep they hoped beyond hope that they were right.

CHAPTER 25
Up and Away

MONDAY, 23RD DECEMBER

Ethan woke first that morning; he had dropped off quite quickly so was fully rested. He waited for his morning drowsiness to fade before heading over to Abi's bed to look out of the window. The village was buzzing with activity, he had never seen so many elves. It was just before seven o'clock and the factory was not yet open.

'Wakey wakey!' he shouted. He was proud as punch that he was awake first for a change and wasn't going to miss the opportunity to let them know it.

'Ethan!' shouted Abi, who was trying to get an extra few minutes sleep. Jack laughed, he could see how irritated Abi was; it was probably more to do with the pending flight than anything else. It wasn't long before all three of the children were up and dressed. Abi was wearing several layers, clearly worried at the elements she was going to be exposed to. They headed downstairs where they were greeted by a fresh-faced Sue and an excited Max. The children hadn't noticed his absence upstairs, but he was now back to the Max of old, full of beans and finally over his mini hibernation.

'Morning you three,' she said. 'We've just been out to get some breakfast for you,' she added patting Max on the head. The children had noticed she was wearing her coat and that Max's feet were covered in snow. They were grateful for Sue's efforts.

'Oh you shouldn't have,' said Abi.

'Well, today's a big day, you can't expect to work on an empty stomach.' Her demeanour was even more positive than normal. Ever since the children had arrived they had noticed how positive and jolly everyone was, but today they had gone into overdrive.

The three of them sat down to breakfast with Sue, but Jack noticed Bernard was missing.

'Where's Bernard?' he asked.

'He's just making some final preparations,' replied Sue. 'He'll be back soon enough'.

The children took their time enjoying yet another of Sue's magnificent meals; it was approaching half past seven when Bernard returned.

'Hello, hello?' he said as he walked through the front door.

'In here darling,' called Sue.

'Look at you three all bright-eyed and fluffy-tailed,' he said to the children as he entered the kitchen.

'Are we all set?' he asked them, looking in particular at Abi. They all nodded, their mouths still full of food.

'Good, good,' he replied. 'We'll head out in about ten minutes.'

After finishing their food the children returned to the bedroom to gather what items they needed. Abi had no idea what to take with her so she decided that it was better to be safe than sorry and decided to take her entire pack. The boys really did not need that much. Ethan decided to take his tablet with him, although this was hardly unusual as it hardly ever left his side for more than ten minutes at a time.

The children returned downstairs to the hall where Bernard and Sue were waiting. Max was turning and turning in circles clearly excited at the prospect of another walk.

'OK, we all set?' asked Bernard. The children all nodded, they appeared nervous, Abi especially.

Bernard opened the door and led the party out into the village square. A large crowd had gathered and started to applaud the group. The children felt ten feet tall, all these kind people were applauding them and it felt like a reward for all of their efforts in returning the Calendar to its rightful home. Ethan decided to acknowledge the crowd and gave some crazy form of royal wave. Jack couldn't let this pass.

'Ha, ha, Ethan you idiot,' he said to his brother, who quickly realised how daft he had just looked and was overcome with embarrassment. Abi chuckled to herself, for a split second she had forgotten her impending departure.

Sue put her arm around Ethan, 'Don't listen to them,' she said, trying to reassure Ethan. 'You wave away,' she added as she raised her own hands to acknowledge the crowd, more to please Ethan than anything else.

Jack noticed that they were heading back towards the main entrance where they had met the elves just two nights ago.

'Where are we going?' he asked.

'Just a little bit further,' replied Bernard. 'Just to the path.' Jack and the other two weren't really clear what he meant and why they were heading that way, but it would soon become obvious. They arrived at the village entrance and the crowd by now was dense. Clearly this is where almost the entire village had gathered and they could soon see why.

'Wow,' said Ethan as he saw the sleigh Bernard had prepared which had eight reindeer harnessed to it. Jack noticed that one reindeer in particular wasn't present.

'Where's Rudolph?' he asked Bernard.

'He hasn't set foot in the village since Santa disappeared,' he replied. 'It's almost as if he's been searching for him.' The villagers believed that Rudolph felt a sense of responsibility for what happened all those years ago and had almost been in a self-imposed exile ever since.

'Oh that's so sad,' said Abi as she listened in to Jack and Bernard's conversation.

The reindeer and the sleigh were facing directly up the path that the children had followed from the Mystic Forest. It now became clear that this long and straight path was to be used as some sort of runway. Mrs Claus was standing beside the sleigh and beckoned Abi over. Abi was hesitant and she turned to her brothers.

'Take care of Max,' she said. 'And tell Mum and Dad I love them.' The boys looked at her confused.

'Tell them yourself,' said Jack. He held no fear for Abi's impending trip, he was one hundred per cent confident in Bernard and Mrs Claus. Ethan had felt confident until, that is, Abi spoke. He ran to his sister and gave her a huge hug. Abi was initially shocked but then squeezed her brother back.

'Everything will be fine, don't you worry,' said Mrs Claus as she hugged the pair of them together.

'Now let's get moving,' she added. With that Bernard bid Sue farewell and climbed on board the sleigh. He sat on the front bench and Mrs Claus and Abi sat on the bench behind. Abi was amazed at how comfortable and almost cosy the sleigh felt. Mrs Claus placed a large blanket across their laps; it was remarkably warm and Abi sunk a little lower to leave just her head exposed to the cold air. She felt incredibly warm and snug.

With a slight tug on the reins Bernard ushered the reindeer to move. They started off at a walk which built into a gentle trot and then finally into a full canter. The sleigh was dragged smoothly across the snow-covered path until finally the reindeer had gathered enough speed and they started to lift, two at a time until all eight and finally the sleigh were airborne.

The elves and Jack and Ethan cheered loudly as the sleigh took off and they waved vigorously at their departing friends. Back on board Abi hadn't moved a muscle, she had felt her stomach move as the sleigh left the ground but her eyes had remained tightly shut. Mrs Claus reached across and placed her hand on Abi's, this instantly relaxed her and she slowly opened her eyes. She was in awe of what she could now see, they were heading towards the Mystic Forest, high above the path and the view was truly amazing. Abi was suddenly grateful that she had been chosen to make this journey with Bernard and Mrs Claus.

Back in the village Sue led the two boys and Max up towards Patrick in the Nav Centre, who was waiting for them on the balcony that surrounded the centre. They were hoping to play a large part in this mission and were keen to assist in any way they could.

'Morning boys. Come inside, let's keep an eye on those three,' Patrick said referring to the sleigh and its passengers. Patrick stopped and looked at Max who was standing alongside Ethan.

'This is Max,' said Ethan as he introduced his dog.

'Hi Max,' said Patrick looking slightly confused.

'He'll be as good as gold,' said Jack. 'Don't you worry.'

The boys keenly shook hands with Patrick and followed him into his futuristic domain.

CHAPTER 26
A Maiden Voyage

MONDAY, 23RD DECEMBER

Jack and Ethan were dumbstruck at the sight of the control centre or Nav Centre as Patrick called it. The technology inside was mind blowing; there were touch screens everywhere, 3D displays left, right and centre. Ethan's tablet now appeared prehistoric with its somewhat limited capabilities.

'I ask just one thing,' said Patrick, 'please try not to touch anything unless you check with me first.'

He was very possessive of his equipment; the entire centre was his absolute pride and joy. Jack was not quite the technology enthusiast that Ethan was, but even he was in awe of what stood before him. Ethan was in his element, he scoured the centre like the proverbial kid in a candy shop.

Patrick focused on the large touch display in the centre of the room. This was what he would use to monitor Bernard and his passengers. It was like a form of futuristic Google Earth Display, but far more advanced and in real time. It was difficult for the children to determine whether this was indeed technology or simply some form of magic.

'How does this even work?' asked a confused Jack. 'I've never seen anything like it.'

Patrick paused for a moment before answering.

'To be honest I'm not exactly sure how he made it, but I sure know how to work it,' he attempted to explain.

'Santa made it?' asked Ethan.

'That's right, he can make pretty much anything he needs,' Patrick replied.

Ethan and Jack were totally confused, not only was this whole centre filled to the rafters with technology beyond their comprehension, but it had been made over at least thirty years ago.

'So Santa made this just before he disappeared?' asked Jack.

'Evan a little before that,' replied Patrick.

'Amazing!' said Ethan. The boys would often hear stories from their father of old Spectrum and Commodore computers of the early eighties, but these pre-dated them, clearly they had been made using some form of alternative technology or even magic of sorts.

'Look, their tracking signal has initiated,' Patrick said pointing to the display. The boys moved closer and leant over the screen.

Back on board the sled Abi was slowly acclimatising to her surroundings. The initial shock of the take-off had started to fade and she had lowered the blanket ever so slightly. Mrs Claus was totally at ease on the sleigh, even though this was her maiden flight she had total faith in Bernard and this was starting to rub off on Abi.

'Doesn't the forest look beautiful?' she said to Abi. Abi looked out to the right side and could see the tops of the forest trees some hundred feet or so below. Through the trees she could see the forest floor which was lush with green pines, just as she had witnesses a few days ago. Abi was surprised at how low they were flying, she had travelled overseas several times with her family and was no stranger to flying, but this was an entirely different experience. Clearly they had no need of climbing to commercial flight heights, and as a result the views on their journey were quite astonishing.

In no time at all they had passed over the Mystic Forest and were almost at the end of Brennin Forest as well until the path that Fang had traversed lay ahead.

'We came this way,' said Abi to Mrs Claus.

'That's right,' she replied. 'Isn't this where Fang helped you?'

'It is, it is,' said an excited Abi. 'He was amazing, he carried all four of us on his back, just incredible.'

'He has a good heart,' said Mr Claus. 'A good heart indeed.'

Abi remained glued to the side of the sleigh for quite some time, she couldn't take her eyes off the scenery below. They passed over both forests and then climbed steadily to cross over the mountain that had housed the children for a night in Fang's company. The sleigh was covering the children's journey in a fraction of the time, the pace of the reindeer was impressive and Abi was now at ease.

'Will we be crossing over Frozen Claw?' she asked Mrs Claus.

'Will we Bernard?' Mrs Claus said as she forwarded the question.

'Yes, indeed, right over it. In fact Abi we'll be almost tracking your route directly I should think,' replied Bernard as he looked at the route that the display in the front of the sleigh laid out.

Abi sat back in the sled, she had a worried look on her face. Frozen Claw didn't hold good memories for any of the children, primarily the presence of Lupus Grimm. Mrs Claus could see Abi was anxious and knew exactly why.

'We won't be going anywhere near the town itself,' she suggested. 'As for Lupus, well you've got nothing to fear from him while I'm with you.'

Her confidence was reassuring, Mrs Claus had an aura about her and Abi felt sure that she was as good as her word. The terrain heading up to Frozen Claw was amazing, it was so remote, Abi could hardly comprehend that Tiberius had led them across this frozen wasteland. The grand scale of their journey dawned on Abi as she looked for signs of life, but could see nothing but white wherever she looked. They had already covered quite some distance and they had now been travelling for over three hours and it was approaching midday.

'What time do you expect us to get to Willow Cove?' asked Abi, aware that the short winter days meant that the light would start to fade just after half past three.

'It will be sometime in the evening, but don't worry, the boys are quite capable of flying in the dark,' she said referring to the reindeer.

Back in the control tower the boys remained glued to the display, they had been watching the GPS position of the sleigh intently. Patrick had from time to time changed the GPS to a real time image of the sleigh that showed all the passengers clearly. This capability was remarkable even though the boys could not fathom how it was even possible, they were quite happy just to enjoy the show. Occasionally Max would jump up and rest his front legs on the surround of the display, even his expression would change when he caught a glimpse of the sleigh in real time. The boys found it comical and encouraged him to jump up whenever the display changed, much to Patrick's frustration as he didn't appreciate the paw prints.

Jack took out his mobile phone and checked for a signal.

'Did Abs text home last night?' he asked Ethan.

'Not sure,' replied his brother.

'OK, I'll just send something now,' replied Jack and went on to write his parents a small message.

Hi Mum, hi Dad, we hope to head home soon. We're all safe and Max is with us so don't worry. 😊

The boys weren't quite as conscious of their parent's obvious worries but they still new that the occasional text was certain to help.

The sleigh was finally approaching Frozen Claw. Abi had hoped that they would perhaps avoid flying directly over the town or avoid it altogether. Hopefully they were in no danger flying a hundred feet or so above the high street but Abi still felt apprehensive.

'Don't worry,' said Mrs Claus. 'This town isn't all bad you know.' Abi then remembered what the Calendar had revealed to them, a cosy and inviting place. Mrs Claus went on to describe to Abi how Frozen Claw once was and she hoped would become again in the future. They were flying over The Broken Sled and towards the train station when Abi became aware of the locals filling the street below. The silence was broken by a cheer, then another, and the cheers grew until there was a loud roar coming from the village. The sight of the sleigh flying overhead was something that the locals hadn't seen for many years and was a very welcome sight indeed. It offered hope to the town and all its inhabitants – well almost all. Mrs Claus noticed Abi suddenly ducking under the blanket.

'What is it dear?' she asked, but as she herself looked over the edge of the sleigh it became obvious, Lupus Grimm was standing by the entrance to the station with a number of his henchmen and two of his hounds with a face like thunder. The sight of a sleigh overhead suggested his days intimidating everyone may be numbered and he was clearly agitated. He began waving his fist in anger, but the sleigh and its passengers were out of his miserable reach.

Mrs Claus put a reassuring arm around Abi, clearly this despicable character made her uncomfortable and she needed comforting. Soon enough the sleigh had passed over the station and made its way out of the town. Finally Abi was able to relax.

She reached into her coat pocket to retrieve her mobile as she wanted to send a message before the signal of Frozen Claw became too weak. Unaware of Jack's message Abi contacted home.

Hi Mum and Dad. We've all had a good night's sleep and are planning our trip back. We won't be away too long now. We all miss you. Love Abi xx 😊

With Frozen Claw disappearing into the distance Abi knew that they were now heading along the route that the Polar Express had taken and in just a few hours she would be once again approaching Willow Cove. Suddenly she felt her heart fill with excitement.

CHAPTER 27
Willow Cove Bound

MONDAY, 23RD DECEMBER

It had now been six days since the children had left and Mum and Dad were helpless, all they had to comfort them was the occasional text and a solitary phone call from their missing children. The police were keeping positive due to the regular contact but were also concerned by the lack of any physical evidence of the children.

Mike had barely left the family home ever since he first arrived and his computer technician had also been ever present. They had a colleague who had visited Frozen Claw, but had just missed the children and that was as far as their search had gone.

This morning though they had received two text messages, both very similar in content but with one big difference, one which the children hadn't accounted for.

'They're not together anymore?' asked Mum.

Mike had explained how the two text messages had come from different locations, the first was from an area to the northwest of Frozen Claw, which could not be pinpointed exactly due to some sort of GPS block that covered the area. The other had come a little later, but this time from just south of Frozen Claw.

'It looks that way,' replied Mike at he consulted with his technician.

Mum turned to Dad looking anxious. He wasn't sure how to respond. Why would they split up, he thought, what purpose would that serve? Mike, however, was more positive.

'Well, at least it suggests they're coming home, or at least some of them,' he suggested. Clearly the second signal was heading closer to home and that had to be good news.

'Just a second Mike,' said the technician as he beckoned Mike over.

'What is it? What is it?' asked Mum frantically.

Mike and the technician looked at the laptop they were using before

Mike turned to Mum.

'The signal is stable,' he said.

'What does that mean?' asked Dad as he sat down beside his wife.

'That means we can track it,' replied Mike, 'and hopefully intercept them.'

Mum squeezed Dad's hand tightly as she looked at him. This was the most positive news they had received since their disappearance. Surely an end to this horrible saga was in sight for the desperate parents.

The sleigh and its passengers were making good progress, they were currently climbing over the mountain that the Polar Express had ascended some days ago. Abi was disappointed that they were not being treated to the spectacle of the Northern Lights again. She explained to Mrs Claus how they had been in awe of the aurora the previous week.

'We're very fortunate to get regular views of that,' replied Mrs Claus. 'It truly is one of the wonders of the world and I can see why so many people travel just to see it.'

'Do they really?' asked Abi.

'Yes, yes, people come from all over the world to get a glimpse of it. Sometimes they can wait for weeks and sometimes they go home empty-handed,' she explained. 'But those of us who are lucky enough to live in the far north, we're a little bit spoilt.'

The sleigh finally crossed over the peak of the mountain and Abi could see down below the huge frozen lake that they had somehow crossed. The Polar Express had indeed completed a remarkable journey to transport them to Frozen Claw and looking back over the route as she was now doing, the journey seemed even more improbable to Abi.

The reindeer headed down sharply towards the lake, levelling out just some fifty feet or so above its frozen surface. The wind chill coming up from the ice forced Abi to retreat below her blanket a little and Mrs Claus chuckled.

'Quite a chill coming up from this lake,' she said as she looked at Abi who by now was barely peeping out from the blanket. Remarkably the cold failed to penetrate through to her at all, this blanket appeared to have some exceptional or even magical properties. Not for the first time on this quest was Abi pleasantly surprised.

The reindeer made light work of crossing the lake. Unlike the heavy locomotive that had the constant worry of the ice beneath it failing, the reindeer flew silently over its surface occasionally lowering so that the sled itself gently brushed the surface of the lake. Abi thoroughly enjoyed this leg of the journey and had grown extremely confident in Bernard and the reindeer, giving out the occasional 'woohoo' as the sleigh skimmed the surface.

The sleigh approached the end of the lake as snow began to fall, lightly at first but then the shower became very heavy indeed. The reindeer lifted the sled slightly higher, high enough to ensure they would not come across any unwanted obstructions. Bernard wrapped another scarf around his neck and donned his goggles. They were an old leather pair, not exactly a fashion statement, but very practical and sturdy; Mrs Claus pulled her coat tight and rolled her hat a little further down her head.

Once they had traversed the lake they were then travelling above some very rough terrain separated by the occasional woodland. The snowfall had not eased at all and it was very difficult for Abi to see anything of the landscape as they passed over it. It was now approaching four o'clock and the light had begun to fade. Abi found it hard to believe how quickly the time had passed, but with all the excitement of a maiden voyage coupled with the amazing scenery she was being exposed to, time had ironically flown by.

Back in Willow Cove Mum and Dad were growing more hopeful by the minute as the GPS track on Abi's phone was still strong and now appeared to show that indeed she or perhaps all of them were returning home. Mike had been making arrangements for them to be intercepted by numerous police officers in their patrol cars. Mike's plan was to simply monitor the signal as long as it was shown to be heading in their direction, however, if they appeared to change direction or head for another location then the officers were instructed to head off and intercept the signal.

Bernard was continuously having to wipe his onboard navigation screen as the snow was relentless. It wasn't long, however, before they could see some lights in the distance. These were not the lights of Willow Cove but instead the bright lights of London. Struggling with the snow, Bernard decided to head towards the city, this was only a slight diversion and he would not have the worries of traffic congestion to deal with at two hundred feet. Braving the cold and the conditions Abi was determined not to miss this unique view of her favourite city, she sat upright clinging onto her blanket. They approached the city from the north and before long were passing over the city centre. All the famous landmarks were covered in a blanket of snow, the Houses of Parliament, Big Ben and Buckingham Palace, even the London Eye was closed due to the extreme winter conditions. The city itself though was not asleep, cars still braved the snowy conditions and even several buses were running.

Abi's delight at the views was matched by Mrs Claus. Abi had forgotten that she too had never travelled on this sleigh and had certainly never seen a city from this perspective before. Abi decided to give Mrs Claus a virtual tour; her knowledge on London and its landmarks was exceptional. Abi dreamed of living in the city and one day she surely would.

Once they had crossed the city centre and Bernard had recalibrated his journey, they headed south towards Willow Cove. The village itself was only about sixty miles out of the city by road, but as the crow flies was only about forty or so miles.

'Not far now,' yelled Bernard as he turned around, his face covered in snow, he looked like a talking snowman Abi thought.

Abi had a little chuckle to herself, at the same time she reached for Mrs Claus' hand, excited at the prospect of reaching Willow Cove. They were now less than an hour away and Mrs Claus too was excited and somewhat nervous about reaching their destination. Was this a wild goose chase, she thought to herself, or was this something much, much more?

Mike stood outside the front of the house talking to several officers, there were six or seven police cars waiting in the street. The plan was for them to intercept Abi and whoever else was travelling with her on the north side of the town near the outskirts of the village. Mike was clear that he didn't want them to be alarmed by a police presence so asked all the officers to ensure their flashing lights were switched off.

Mike led the way with Mum and Dad in the back of the car on an unofficial ride along. He took the convoy up to a T-junction on the north side of the village where the village road met the main A-road leading both north and south. The cars spread out slightly, positioning themselves on the roadside but leaving plenty of room for traffic to pass. In the passenger seat was Mike's dedicated technician who had been a real rock for the parents during this whole affair, his laptop had been replaced with a tablet. Some of the other officers too had been provided with equipment to follow the signal emitting from Abi's phone.

'Any second now,' he said as the moving image approached their destination on the map.

'And… go, go, go,' said Mike. All the police cars headlights were turned on and several of the officers got out of their vehicles and shone their torches down the road. Nothing, they were greeted with nothing, just empty roads as far as their headlights could stretch. Not a sign of anyone, no cars, no pedestrians, although that was unlikely in these conditions.

Dad opened the back door of the car and stepped out.

'Well, where are they?' he asked Mike.

Mike popped his head back through his window, looking at his technician for answers. The technician shrugged his shoulders, 'I don't understand,' he said, 'they came right towards us, the signal was so strong.'

There was a lot of posturing and a lot of confused faces before Mike made a decision.

'Right,' he started. 'I'll drop you two at home and head down to the station to check the signal on the station system.' He instructed two of the cars to stay at the junction and asked the others to trawl the village looking for any sign of the children. Unknown to Mum, Dad and Mike, Abi had in fact passed directly over them just some hundred feet or so above, but in the heavy snow the sleigh passed by undetected. Abi had indeed arrived back at Willow Cove.

CHAPTER 28
A Reunion

MONDAY, 23RD DECEMBER

'Which way Abi?' asked Bernard as the sleigh approached the town square.

'It's up behind the library,' she replied pointing to the large library that stood in the square. It was still very difficult for Bernard to see clearly and there didn't appear to be anywhere obvious to land. Rooftops were a little too treacherous in these harsh conditions. He circled the square several times trying to spot an adequate landing strip.

Abi was of little use, she wasn't exactly sure what Bernard needed in terms of a landing strip and didn't want to suggest somewhere that may not have been suitable. Then she had a thought.

'Bernard?' she called out through the snow.

'What is it Abi?' he replied not turning round this time as he desperately searching for somewhere to land.

'Would a football field work?' she asked.

'Yes, yes, which way?' he replied hurriedly.

Abi directed Bernard down the path towards the beach and pointed out the football field alongside the town's leisure centre. Bernard was happy with their choice and he made quick work of guiding the reindeer down safely and bringing the sleigh to rest almost on the half way line. Abi was conscious that people in the village knew she was missing and would be looking out for her. She pointed this out to Mrs Claus and Bernard, but regardless they decided she should accompany Mrs Claus to Old Kris' house.

The three of them stepped down and out of the sleigh. Bernard tended to the reindeer as Mrs Claus and Abi headed off up the path back towards the town.

'Watch this path it's always very slippery,' said Abi.

'Thank you, Abi, but I'm sure I'll be fine,' replied Mrs Claus, who after years in the far north was accustomed to such conditions. They were approaching the square when Abi could see car lights approaching; she ducked down between two houses leaving Mrs Claus to continue alone. The car was one of the police cars and it drove towards Mrs Claus. The officer shone his torch, almost rudely, in her direction. The car slowed slightly before the officer's gaze left Mrs Claus and they continued to search the village.

Abi popped her head out, 'Have they gone?'

'Yes, it's safe,' replied Mrs Claus. Abi caught her up and they entered the square. They made sure to stick close to the buildings to stay out of sight as much as possible. Old Kris lived up a small path behind the library and Abi led the way. Just over half way up the path Mrs Claus' pace picked up and she walked past Abi; she was soon in sight of the house and she stopped in her tracks. The look and the aura of the house immediately struck her, it seemed eerily familiar.

Abi stopped behind her.

'What is it?' she asked.

'I'm not sure,' she replied. 'But something feels so familiar here.'

Inside the house Old Kris was sitting down enjoying some cocoa when a strange feeling overcame him, almost as if someone was calling out his name. He stood up and moved towards the window.

Mrs Claus was walking very slowly towards the house, her hands were shaking and her legs felt strangely numb. Kris pulled back his curtains inside the house and peered through the window. Through the snow he caught sight of her, his heart felt like it was going to leap out of his chest. He let the curtain go, his breath became short, his heart was racing at a million miles an hour, his brain was going into overdrive as some memories were starting to come back.

He knew this woman, he was sure he did, her name … Jessica, it came to him. He had visions of Santa's village, visions of elves and small cosy cottages. Mrs Claus had reached his porch and Old Kris walked towards his front door, he opened the door slowly and stepped out onto the porch.

The years had not aged him much but it was such a long time ago that Mrs Claus wasn't one hundred per cent certain.

'Kris?' she asked.

There was a pause. Old Kris then stepped forward towards Mrs Claus.

'Jessica?' he responded. Mrs Claus' heart filled with emotion, she threw her arms around Old Kris and burst into tears. With that embrace, everything came flooding back to him. His head was like a firework going off, thousands of memories came flooding back until he was almost overloaded with information.

He leant back to take a closer look at his wife.

'Oh Jessica,' he said, 'how I've missed you.' The years had been confusing for Kris, his memories erased but his lonely existence had been difficult for him. The villagers' welcoming nature had been his only consolation.

'My darling Kris,' she said. 'I thought I'd lost you forever.' She embraced her long lost husband once more.

Behind Mrs Claus, Abi stood in floods of tears.

'Whatever is the matter young lady?' asked Santa.

'Nothing,' she replied wiping away her tears. 'It's just so....' She couldn't finish her sentence because she was so choked up with emotion.

'I know, I know,' responded Mrs Claus as she stepped down to comfort Abi, let's head inside.'

'Of course, of course,' said Kris.

The three of them entered Santa's cosy home from home. Mrs Claus was intrigued as to how her husband had spent the past thirty or so years. There were so many questions she had and so many questions Santa needed answering. The reunited couple sat down on the sofa next to each other while Abi sat on one of the remaining armchairs. The two of them hardly took a breath for the next ten minutes or so, asking question after question, desperate to make up for lost time.

'Where are my manners?' said Santa as he looked over at Abi. 'Let me make us all a drink.' He headed off to the kitchen before returning a few minutes later with some drinks. The next hour was filled with talk of Christmases past and how Mrs Claus had kept the village and the workshops going for all these years. Santa still didn't have much recollection of the crash itself, but even those memories were starting to return piece by piece.

Santa was keen to know what part Abi had played in all of this and she happily gave a full account of the children's quest, even reminding him of the visit they had paid him just over a week ago.

'Of course, you were with your brothers if I remember,' he said.

'Yes, yes, they love your cocoa,' she replied.

'So where are they now?' he asked. Mrs Claus went on to explain how the boys were still in Santa's village and how the elves were aware of her journey and were waiting for any news with bated breath. After finishing their drinks and talking some more Mrs Claus made a suggestion.

'We need to get back Kris,' she said.

'Back?' he asked.

'Yes, back to the village,' she replied.

'Yes, yes, but how…?' he paused.

'Bernard's on the football pitch,' said Abi, clearly understanding what was confusing Santa.

'Bernard, really? Is he here with you?' he asked.

Clearly he was delighted to hear that his faithful friend was with them and the three of them made moves to leave. Santa fetched one or two items from upstairs, he knew he would be back and have time to clear out his home, but there were one or two items he wanted to bring.

Santa put out his log fire and led them all out of the house not stopping to lock the door, Abi pointed this out to him.

'Old habits die hard,' he said looking at Mrs Claus and chuckling.

The three of them made their way uninterrupted down the path and across the square. The path down to the football pitch was even more treacherous downhill and Abi had to keep her wits about her to stay upright. Mr and Mrs Claus, however, were oblivious to the conditions underfoot and talked continuously.

'Santa?' someone called as they reached the edge of the football pitch. Bernard was running across the pitch his arms help out in front of him.

'It's really you, it really is!' he said as he greeted his long lost friend with a huge hug.

'You've put on a bit of weight,' joked Santa as he hugged his friend back.

'I can't believe it, I really can't, wait until the others know,' he said.

Behind Santa, Bernard could see some lights starting to come down the road behind them. It was the police who were still desperately searching the town.

'We need to get moving and quickly,' said Bernard pointing at the lights that would come round the corner at any moment. Abi was first on board and quickly under her blanket. Mrs Claus climbed in alongside her and Santa sat up front with Bernard.

The police car came slowly around the corner and stopped, both its light pointing at the sleigh and its passengers. The officers inside did a double take, they could hardly believe what they were looking at, believing it must be some practical joke. Bernard pulled hard on the reins and the reindeer headed straight for the end of the football pitch and directly at the police car. The officers looked at each other in utter confusion, frozen with uncertainty. They watched helplessly as the reindeer galloped towards them before finally lifting off the ground as they reached the car park at the end of the pitch.

'Ho, ho,' laughed Santa as the sleigh left the ground, that was one sensation that he hadn't felt in a long time.

CHAPTER 29
Flying Home for Christmas

MONDAY, 23RD TUESDAY, 24TH DECEMBER

Patrick was on a handset speaking to Bernard while the boys were playing some Christmas video game Patrick had shown them on one of the other displays in the Nav Centre. He had promised Bernard that he wouldn't tell the elves of their news, he hadn't, however, promised not to tell the boys.

'They're on their way back,' he said.

The boys paused their game and looked at each other before Jack asked, 'How many of them?' Patrick was unable to conceal his excitement.

'All four of them, all four, Santa's coming home, he's finally coming home!' he yelled as he jogged around the central console waving his hands in the air.

Jack pumped his fist, 'I knew it. I knew it!' he said. Ethan was hysterical as he watched Patrick's celebration dance.

'Tomorrow will be hectic, it will be mad, the presents will have to go,' said Patrick, as much to himself as to the boys. It would be the 24th in less than five hours and Santa would need to work his magic to ensure things were delivered on time.

Back in Willow Cove Mum and Dad were at home when Mike returned.

'Any sign, is there any sign?' asked Mum.

'I'm afraid not,' replied Mike, 'but....'

'What is it?' asked Mum.

Mike explained what his officers had seen, or at least thought they had seen, down near the football pitch. He explained that this coincided with the GPS tracker showing that Abi once again appeared to be heading away from the town. Mum and Dad didn't know what to make of this information, nothing was making much sense anymore.

It had dawned on Dad how much the children had been asking about Christmas and how they had found a few things in Abi's bedroom the morning they left. He pointed this out to his wife after Mike had left and wondered what his wife would make of it.

'What do you think?' he asked, '...and that survey they seemed to be completing.' Dad was trying to make sense of this whole drama and, unknown to the them, he was making quite a fist of the detective work.

'I don't know Josh, it's all a bit weird. It's all getting a little bit crazy now if I'm to be honest,' she replied.

'Well, the far north thing would seem to fit as well,' he added.

Mum was shattered, she had hardly slept for the past week. She was totally confused by the conflicting stories she was getting and decided that she needed some sleep to try and make sense of things. Dad agreed and the two of them went for a very early night.

The sleigh by now was airborne and making light work of the poor weather. The reindeer had appeared to respond to the return of their leader and were making astonishing progress on their return home. It was barely six or seven hours before they were flying quietly over the Mystic Forest and making their way towards Santa's village. Abi had slept virtually the whole way back, the emotion of the occasion had worn her out and her head was resting on Mrs Claus' lap.

Mrs Claus rocked her gently.

'Wake up dear, we're nearly home,' she said.

'Mum?' mumbled Abi in her sleepy state.

'No dear,' said Mrs Claus with a little laugh, 'it's me Jessica.'

Abi rubbed her eyes, 'Oh, sorry,' she said a little embarrassed.

In the village Patrick had sent word of the sleigh's imminent return. He had made no mention of who would be returning, but regardless of that and the early hour – it was now just after one o'clock – the elves had started to flow out of their cottages and a large crowd was starting to form at the entrance to the village.

Santa sat proudly in the front of the sleigh. He had taken the reins from Bernard as they passed Frozen Claw as he was eager to renew his acquaintance with the reindeer and the sleigh. He gave a flick of the reins with his hands, which signalled the reindeer to start their descent. They were now running above the path that had led the children from the Mystic Forest.

The reindeer started, two by two to land on the path until all eight were finally grounded and trotting steadily. The sleigh then caressed the floor gently as it landed and continued on down the path. Santa had lost none of his skills, the memory of that incident all those years ago had played on Santa's mind as he led the sleigh down towards the path.

They were still a couple of hundred yards from the village entrance and the elves now numbered almost a thousand. They were all peering desperately through the snowfall to try and see exactly who they were going to greet. Patrick, the boys and Max had now joined the crowd and were standing near the front with Sue.

One elf suddenly shouted out, 'It's Santa, it's Santa,' as he caught a glimpse of his hero, his leader, as the sleigh approached. The elves started to become animated, looking around to see each other's faces.

'It is, it is!' shouted another. The sleigh was by now in full sight, there could be no doubt that Santa was back and the crowd roared with delight. Elves were high-fiving each other, hugging each other, there were tears of joy and songs started to ring around the crowd.

The sleigh slowly came to a halt just a few yards from the crowd. Max was a little caught up in the emotion and ran full pelt to greet the travellers, but as only Max could do, he lost his footing and slid directly below the sled and came out the other side. He jumped to his feet and tried to get going again but his feet were unable to grip the frozen ground. It was comical watching him put so much effort into his running but getting nowhere. Then he finally fell in a heap and gave up. The crowd roared with laughter. Abi climbed down from the side of the sleigh and went round to help her struggling pet.

'Oh, Max, what are we going to do with you,' she said.

Santa sat in the sleigh looking at the welcoming crowd that had gathered with a tear in his eye. He stood up in the sleigh, ready to address his audience. There was a long pause, the crowd quietened before he spoke, 'Hello once again my loyal friends. This day has been a long time coming. There is so much I would like to tell you and so many questions I have to ask, but as you are all aware it is now just after one o'clock in the morning and today is Christmas Eve,' he paused as they all cheered.

He held both his hands up to ask the crowd to be quiet. 'I've spoken to Bernard and he assures me you've all been busy making preparations.' The crowd was full of anticipation, they almost knew what was coming next. 'This year, we will make our deliveries. This year the world will have a Christmas once again,' he said raising a closed fist into the air.

The crowd went ballistic, everything they had spent over thirty years waiting for had returned, Santa was back and so was Christmas. Santa climbed down from the sleigh and walked through the crowd. He gave Sue a big hug and then shook hands and hugged many of the gathered elves. He made his way through to the town square where he stopped and called together all his factory managers. They assured him that production was complete and that everything was in place for him to set off within an hour or two. Bernard was quick to tend to the herd and took them back to the stable for a well-earned rest, they only had a couple of hours to recoup but he was sure they were up to the task.

The crowd of elves were returning from the main entrance towards the square when they suddenly parted leaving a clear walkway between them. Santa turned, not sure exactly what was happening. The elves had seen a reindeer approaching down the path and had made room for their incoming guest. The reindeer walked slowly and nervously between the crowd and towards the square.

Santa's face lit up.

'Rudi!' he yelled and with that the reindeer darted towards his beloved master. Unlike Max he was anything but clumsy and stopped just inches from Santa and proceeded to almost lick him to death.

Santa chuckled as he embraced his trusty steed. Rudolph had spent years in the wilderness looking for his lost leader and now his search was over.

'Well, Rudi?' asked Santa. 'Are you up for this?' Rudolph stamped his two front hoofs on the floor, a clear indication that he was ready once again to lead Santa's sleigh.

Bernard returned to the square and was delighted to see Rudolph being greeted back into the fold. He would be refreshed and ready to lead the reindeer tonight and this was music to Bernard's ears.

Sue led the three children back into her cottage and asked them to take a seat in the lounge. They sat patiently, they were all exhausted, even Abi after her mid-air sleep was feeling shattered. They heard the door open in the hall and a couple of familiar voices. Mrs Claus and Santa entered the room.

'So these are your brothers Abi?' he asked.

'Yes, this is Jack and this is Ethan,' she said as she introduced her siblings. Santa took a seat as he addressed the three of them.

'You have no idea how much you have done for us,' he started. 'The journey that you undertook to return my Calendar and to ultimately reunite me with my wife is incredible. For three young children to brave the perils of such a journey is just remarkable. I will be forever in your debt. Not to mention the millions of children across the world whose lives will change as of today.'

The children looked a little embarrassed at receiving all this praise, they in truth had no idea the impact their astonishing journey would have on the rest of the world. Santa Claus had been found and the pain of all those who had mourned Christmas was about to be eased.

'Now, if you'll excuse me I have a busy night ahead. I suggest you three get some sleep, we will need to ensure your safe return home as soon as you are rested,' he said. 'But rest assured, this is not the last you'll see of this village, you are welcome here anytime and I know that Bernard and Sue extend that welcome as well.'

'Of course, of course,' said Sue, 'there will always be a home from home for you here.'

Abi could feel herself getting emotional, this felt like goodbye. She stood up and ran over to Mrs Claus to give her a huge hug. Ethan was also caught up in the moment and likewise ran over to Sue. Jack tried to keep his composure and walked over to Santa and offered his hand. Santa obliged and gave Jack a firm handshake.

'Thank you once again young man,' he said placing a hand on his shoulder. He could see Jack was struggling to hold his emotions together.

Santa rose from his chair and made his way towards the front door. He stopped and turned to speak to Ethan.

'Could I ask one final favour of you master Ethan?' he said.

Ethan finally let go of Sue and stood looking at Santa.

'I could do with using that tablet of yours tonight if that would be OK?' asked Santa.

Ethan was a little confused, after seeing all the technology that Patrick had at his disposal he wasn't quite sure how his tablet would help, but he was quite willing to let Santa have it.

'Sure,' he said shrugging his shoulders and returning to the sofa to collect it.

'I'll be sure to return it to you in once piece,' said Santa as he accepted it before leaving through the front door.

Sue and the children stood in the hallway.

'Right, you three, I suggest we all head upstairs, it's been a long day and we all need the rest.'

The children were in no position to argue, they were all out on their feet. They made their way wearily upstairs and collapsed on their beds and very quickly fell into a deep sleep.

CHAPTER 30
The Magic Begins

CHRISTMAS EVE, TUESDAY, 24TH DECEMBER

Santa's arrival in the early hours of Christmas Eve had meant that the elves' plans for Christmas were once again going to be carried out. They were working frantically to ensure they met their target and provided Santa with everything he needed to complete his seemingly impossible task.

The various time zones of the world allowed Santa to travel from continent to continent and from country to country saving time as he went. The magic of Christmas also allowed him the additional time needed to ensure that all his deliveries would be on time.

Santa's sleigh would make journey after journey that day, returning multiple times to collect more gifts for delivery. Fortunately Santa's sleigh was not the only airborne vehicle, there were numerous smaller sleighs pulled by just a pair of reindeer, these were ridden by some of the elder elves from the village. Such a huge logistical challenge meant that all hands were on pump for the duration of Christmas Eve. Patrick's Nav centre was crucial to this challenge and he revelled in the complexity of the operation. To anyone else the vast array of displays and GPS equipment would be mind-boggling, but to Patrick this was everything he wanted, he was in his element.

The children slept until well into the afternoon and were well rested by the time Sue called up to the room.

'Hello?' she said as she knocked on the door.

Abi stretched out as she woke.

'Hello Sue, what time is it?' she asked.

'Just after two o'clock,' replied Sue.

'Ooops!' said Abi a little embarrassed.

'You all deserve it,' said Sue as she looked at Abi and the now waking boys.

'Has Santa gone?' asked Ethan

'Yes, he'll be out all day you can be sure of that,' said Sue.

Jack climbed out of bed and headed over to the window. He was surprised at how quiet everything seemed outside.

'Where is everyone?' he asked

Sue headed over to take a look. 'Well, I suppose they'll either be in the factory or the warehouse,' she replied.

Jack had expected a bustling village full of activity, but in reality this was a far more ruthless operation that had to be executed with clinical precision. The elves and the village had always come across as laid back and very relaxed, however, this was their main purpose in life and they had to be sure that after all these years that nothing was left to chance.

Patrick was busy monitoring the deliveries in the Nav Centre when he noticed that Santa was returning for another collection but was slightly off track.

'You might want to alter your bearing Santa,' he suggested through the communication system.

'I just have something small to attend to,' replied Santa. 'I'll be back on schedule soon enough.'

Patrick was uncomfortable with this, he liked routine. He liked everything in its place and for plans to be adhered to religiously. He did, however, have total faith in Santa and would allow him to indulge his desire. The one thing that Patrick didn't quite understand though was why Santa needed to revisit Frozen Claw!

The children were by now all dressed and downstairs enjoying a late lunch with Sue. Abi was conscious that their time in the village was coming to an end and they would soon be returning home to Willow Cove.

'Sue?' she asked.

'Yes, dear,' replied Sue.

'When we get home, who can we tell about what has happened?' she asked.

Sue paused for a moment to think before answering.

'Well, I suppose that's up to the three of you,' she said. 'We certainly can't tell you what to do and who to tell, we'll just trust in your judgement. After all, without your help, none of this would have been possible.'

Ethan looked at Abi and just shrugged his shoulders as if to suggest they could just share their adventure with everyone. Deep down, however, Abi knew that the three of them would only share this secret with their very nearest and dearest. The children were also aware of how fanciful this story would appear to everyone, and that only those close to them would probably believe their tale.

Christmas Eve flew past in the village, the elves were predictably nowhere to be seen and the children felt almost disappointed at how uneventful the day was. By the time they had finished their late lunch the light was already fading. It was, however, probably just what they needed, a quiet day of rest and recuperation. After lunch they moved through to the lounge and listened to Sue's stories of Christmases past. Ethan, however, had an important question on his mind.

'When are we going home Sue?' he asked. This was something they hadn't thought to ask since their arrival, they had been in such awe of the village and its inhabitants that they had not dreamt of wanting to leave. However, with the slow pace of the day, Ethan's thoughts had drifted to his hometown and more importantly his parents.

'I can't be sure,' she said, 'but certainly in the next day or two I would imagine.'

'Perhaps I should message Mum and Dad,' said Abi.

'If you like,' replied Sue. 'I can't imagine the worry they've had.'

Abi popped upstairs to the bedroom and sat down on her bed to send what she hoped would be the last message she needed to send her beleaguered parents.

> *Hi Mum and Dad, everything is OK. We've done what we set out to do and will be home in the next couple of days. Can't wait to see you, miss you terribly, love Abi, and Merry Christmas* 😊

Unknown to Abi those final two words were a real comfort to her parents, Dad in particular. He already had his suspicions as to what kind of saga the children were involved in and now for Abi to wish them Merry Christmas only compounded his suspicions.

Later that evening Mrs Claus returned to the cottage to see the children.

'Hi kids,' she said as Sue let her in. The children were waiting in the hall to greet her. She was as ever immaculately dressed and fresh faced.

'I've spoken to Santa and he has suggested that tomorrow we will both take the three of you home to Willow Cove. How does that sound?' she asked.

The children's faces lit up. They didn't want to appear ungrateful for the village's hospitality but this was the longest that they had ever been parted from their parents.

'On the sleigh?' asked Ethan, perhaps he was more excited by the prospect of the flight than returning home.

'Of course,' laughed Mrs Claus.

'Now I know you've done very little today, but it's still important for you to get a good night's sleep tonight as the journey home can be quite emotional and very tiring,' she said.

With that she gave Sue a hug, as if preparing to leave.

'Won't you stay for a drink?' asked Jack. He could sense that their time with these wonderful people was coming to an end and wanted to ensure that every minute was treasured.

Mrs Claus looked at Jack lovingly, he was the last one she expected to be showing any signs of emotion.

'OK Jack, just for a short while,' she said as she removed her coat and walked through to the lounge with the children. Sue went through to the kitchen to make the party a drink. Mrs Claus kept the children entertained for over an hour. They enjoyed her company so much and hung on her every word as she recounted many festive tales.

Mrs Claus finally said her goodnights and left the children in Sue's safe hands.

It was now after nine o'clock and the children were making plans to head up to bed. It had been a very short day but nonetheless the children were keen to get a good night's rest. They thought the sooner they got to sleep the sooner tomorrow would come, true Christmas Eve logic.

That night Sue crept into the room and quietly ensured that the children's bags were packed tidily and that everything was in place for their journey home. An hour or so before midnight Santa knocked quietly at the front door and Sue answered.

'All set?' he asked

'Yes, they're sound asleep,' she replied.

Santa smiled back at Sue before he entered the cottage.

CHAPTER 31
A Perfect Present

CHRISTMAS MORNING, WEDNESDAY, 25TH DECEMBER

Jack was lying in his bed staring up at the ceiling, he wasn't quite sure what time it was or what time they would be leaving. He was so relaxed and didn't want to move, this bunk bed was so comfortable… bunk bed he thought… then where had the top bunk gone? He sat up quickly and looked around frantically, this wasn't the bedroom he'd spent the last few nights in, this was the bedroom he'd spent the last few years in, he was home!

He jumped out of bed and ran out to the familiar landing of his home. He barged into Abi's room, she was fast asleep so he leant over her bed and shook her, gently at first, but then more vigorously as she refused to wake.

'Get off, get off,' she said, almost in her sleep.

'Abs, Abs, we're home!' said Jack.

Abi's eyes opened wide.

'What?' she said.

'We're home!' said Jack

Abi sat up quickly taking in her surroundings

'What?… How?…' she stuttered.

With that Jack ran out of the room and across the hall to Ethan's bedroom. He was already sitting up in his bed with a comical look on his face – confusion, excitement – they were all mixed up in his expression somewhere. Max was lying across Ethan's legs and seemed more relaxed with the situation than any of the children.

Jack pulled Ethan out of the bed and dragged him onto the landing where Abi was standing. They all looked towards their parent's bedroom before bursting in excited to see their Mum and Dad. To their disappointment the bed was empty; no one had slept in it that night; the children were confused.

They looked at each other. It was barely seven o'clock, where could their parents be? The three of them made their way downstairs to the kitchen. It was a bit of a mess, cups and mugs all over the place, the milk was still out on the worktop and the coffee jar had been left open. Abi walked around to look in the lounge, she turned her head to look at her brothers with a huge smile on her face; the boys joined her.

The three of them were looking at their parents who were huddled together on the sofa, very much a couple still in love. Next to the sofa stood a beautifully decorated Christmas tree with presents placed neatly below it. They watched their parents sleeping peacefully for a minute or so before Max came bounding in, rushing up to the sofa. Unusually for Max he gently put his two front paws on the sofa before starting to nuzzle Dad and then licking his owner's cheek softly.

Dad brushed the dog's face away gently, then a second time and finally a third before he opened his eyes. He looked at the three children standing in the archway to the kitchen. His eyes started to fill with tears and he nudged his wife gently.

'Merry Christmas darling,' he said.

She started to stir slowly and squeezed her husband. She opened her eyes and looked at her soul mate, she could see the emotion in his eyes.

'What is it Josh?' she asked, unaware of her children's presence.

He looked at her and repeated himself, 'Merry Christmas,' his eyes returning to the children. Mum turned to see what he was looking at and she was suddenly overcome with emotion. She buried her head in her husband's chest and sobbed. The children were a little confused by her reaction, they had expected her to jump up and run at them with open arms, but this was not a simple case of them returning from a trip, their parents had been in fear of their children's lives. The children could see how upset their parents were and rushed over to them. Abi was crying before she even reached the sofa, Ethan too was like a blubbering wreck. All three children embraced their parents for what seemed like an eternity, Mum and Dad didn't want to let their children go.

Mum wiped Abi's tears from her face and looked at her daughter.

'My Abi', she said. 'My little Abi.' She reached out for her boys in a similar manner. Dad had his hands full with Max trying to climb up onto his lap.

'Merry Christmas Mum and Dad,' said Ethan as he stood up beside the Christmas tree.

Their parents looked at both the tree and Ethan and smiled through their tears of joy.

'What's that?' asked Jack as he heard some commotion outside and he moved to the front window to take a look.

'Come look, come look,' he said as he ran to the front door.

The entire family got up from the sofa. Mum was wiping her eyes trying to make herself presentable. They walked through the hall and outside to the front porch where Jack was standing. It looked as if the entire neighbourhood was out in the street. They were holding presents and hugging each other in celebration.

'Merry Christmas!' shouted one neighbour from across the street, holding his small child in one arm and a present in another. Not only were the locals holding gifts but the street was littered with decorations, tinsel and glitter everywhere, a real festive exhibition.

'Merry Christmas!' shouted mum emotionally. The village was buzzing with excitement. People's prayers from all those years ago had been answered, Christmas had returned, gifts were being shared and for the first time in many years the world was united in one beautiful celebration.

The family stood on that porch for quite some time. The warmth of Christmas spirit sheltered them from the cold. They watched as more and more people filled the street all in total disbelief at what had happened. For all the town's children this was a new experience, but for the parents this was a return to the glory days of Christmases past. Dad finally led the family back inside.

'Now before you share your stories with us, let's just enjoy this day and enjoy each other,' he said.

'Does that mean…?' started Ethan excitedly.

'Yes, let's open the presents,' replied Mum.

With that the children raced over to the tree and started to open their gifts. That morning was one that the family would never forget, they were reunited after one of the most harrowing experiences and Christmas had returned to the world. They spent the morning opening the most wonderful gifts and receiving visits from what seemed like the entire town's population, keen to celebrate the safe return of the children. The family were remarkably fortunate to live in a town with such a strong sense of community spirit. Mum and Dad had received such overwhelming support through their ordeal.

Underneath the tree lay one final present, beautifully gift wrapped, which was addressed to all three of the children. Ethan was allowed to remove the wrapping and to his surprise he found it was his tablet.

'That's strange?' said Ethan quizzically, Jack and Abi just laughed. Mum and Dad weren't in on the joke, so just looked at each other puzzled.

On the front of the tablet was a post-it note with a message on it.

Just a little something to say thank you. Press play.

Ethan powered up the table and noticed it was on a media player; he sat on the sofa and Jack and Abi flanked him. The video started with Bernard and Sue offering a message of thanks and wishing them a Merry Christmas. Then it passed to Mrs Claus and finally to Santa who left the most heartfelt thank you for all the children's efforts and also included Max in his thoughts, to which the dog duly responded with a bark. The video promised the children a lifetime of Christmases and Santa vowed to once again bring joy back into the world. There was then what appeared to be the beginning of a walk-through of a beautifully decorated town, the streets full of festive spirit and people dancing and cheering. This town appeared strangely familiar as did the gentleman that was begrudgingly handing out small gifts outside a tavern, at that point Jack shouted, 'That's Lupus Grimm!'

The children laughed at this once tyrant now handing out presents to the town folk.

With that the footage panned upwards revealing the tavern's name:

The Broken Sled

Christmas had finally returned to Frozen Claw and indeed to the rest of the world, the Patterson family was complete again and Santa's village was back in business.